CAST AWAY

SPELLBOUND PARANORMAL COZY MYSTERY, BOOK 6

ANNABEL CHASE

RED PALM PRESS LLC

Cast Away

A Spellbound Paranormal Cozy Mystery, Book 6

By Annabel Chase

Cover Design by Alchemy

❀ Created with Vellum

CHAPTER 1

"TODAY'S EXERCISE is all about trust," Lady Weatherby said.

"Ugh," Millie muttered. "I hate trust exercises."

"That's because you don't trust anyone," Laurel whispered.

"Witches? Is there something you'd like to share with the class?" Lady Weatherby asked pointedly.

Laurel shook her head, but Millie decided that honesty was the best policy.

"We're with each other all the time," Millie complained. "Obviously, we trust each other. There's no real point to the exercise."

"Just because you spend a lot of time with someone doesn't mean you automatically trust them," Lady Weatherby said. "If you worked next to Jemima every day in Mix-n-Match, for example, would that make you trust her?"

"Definitely not," Begonia said under her breath.

"If nothing else, it's a reinforcement," Lady Weatherby said. "The coven has an annual retreat that involves an entire evening of trust exercises."

Millie gave a disapproving snort. "I think I'll call in sick that day."

"Millie, I think you'll find it's witches like you who need these exercises most of all." Professor Holmes appeared in the back of the classroom.

"Good morning, Professor Holmes," Lady Weatherby greeted him and the rest of the class followed suit.

"I thought I would take part in today's lesson," the kindly wizard said.

"Any particular reason, Professor?" Laurel asked.

He rubbed the back of his head. "Mainly because the cleaning fairies are in my office and there's a plumber pulling apart the kitchen in my house."

"So you seek refuge, is that it?" Lady Weatherby asked, mildly amused.

"There are several coffee shops at your disposal," I said.

Lady Weatherby silenced me with a stern look. "If Professor Holmes would like to join us, then we are more than happy to have him."

Professor Holmes gave a slight nod before joining her at the front of the classroom.

"An ideal partner for this exercise," Lady Weatherby said.

"Indeed." Professor Holmes retrieved his wand. "Shall I demonstrate?"

Lady Weatherby swept back her cloak and moved in front of the desk so that we could all see her. "Professor Holmes will perform a trust spell that lifts me into the air. If I fail to trust him, the spell won't work."

Wow. Lady Weatherby was placing her dignity in the hands of Professor Holmes. I was certain she'd want to be the one to perform the spell. Talk about setting an example.

"Keep in mind that it's a bonding exercise," Professor Holmes said. "Both participants must be fully engaged for the spell to be successful."

"Indeed," Lady Weatherby said. "Whereas much of our magic is one-sided, this particular exercise is not."

Professor Holmes aimed his wand and said, "Our bond lifts you up/My wand lifts you up/Your trust lifts you up."

I watched with interest as Lady Weatherby's feet left the floor and her body began to rise. She was hovering about an inch above the desks when a gust of wind blew open the classroom door, startling everyone.

Professor Holmes jerked his head toward the sound, his attention waning. As a result, Lady Weatherby plunged toward the floor, her cloak billowing on the way down. She managed to stop herself with a single word. I didn't even hear what the word was, only the lash of her sharp tongue and then her feet drifted smoothly to the floor. The intimidating version of Mary Poppins. All that was missing was an umbrella.

"Apologies, Lady Weatherby," Professor Holmes said, slightly ruffled.

Lady Weatherby adjusted her antlered headdress, remaining her usual calm and collected self. "No apology needed, although we must have someone address the issue with that door. It appears to be faulty."

At that moment, Sedgwick careened through the open doorway and perched on a shelf in the back of the room. I slapped my forehead.

Who is she calling faulty? the owl asked.

Sedgwick, what are you doing? You interrupted a spell.

You left me behind this morning. What was that about?

You were asleep. You looked so peaceful. I didn't want to wake you.

I always look peaceful. I'm an adorable owl. Next time wake me.

"Miss Hart," Lady Weatherby's voice interrupted our exchange. "I do believe that is your familiar."

"Yes, Lady Weatherby."

"Please advise Wedgewood…"

"Sedgwick."

She doesn't even know my name? Sedgwick sounded outraged by the slight.

"Please advise Sedgwick that class begins promptly and, if he cannot arrive with you, he should wait outside until class has finished."

Did you hear that? I asked.

I'm mute, not deaf.

Mute? Boy, do I wish that was true.

And be like all the other owls? I don't think you really want that. I'm special.

I rolled my eyes. *If you say so.*

Lady Weatherby smoothed the front of her dark cloak. "Let us try again, shall we?"

Professor Holmes nodded, whatever embarrassment he may have felt quickly subsiding. He pointed his wand and said, "Our bond lifts you up/My wand lifts you up/Your trust lifts you up."

Lady Weatherby's body relaxed as she floated in midair. "Well done, Professor Holmes."

With the flick of his wand, he brought her back to the floor.

"Now who would like to be the first volunteer?" Lady Weatherby addressed the class.

Sophie raised her hand. "I think I was good at these exercises last year." No surprise there. Sophie was sweet and one of the most trusting people I knew.

"You absolutely were," Professor Holmes agreed.

"Almost all of us were," Begonia said. "It was Millie who failed…" Her hand shot across her mouth to prevent herself from saying anything more.

Beside her, Millie stiffened. "I trust everyone, thank you very much. The exercises weren't designed for my type of magic."

"Which type of magic is that exactly?" Lady Weatherby asked. "Witches' magic? Because I can assure you, we're all witches here. Same type of magic."

I slipped down in my seat, guilt overtaking me. They didn't know the truth—that I wasn't a witch. My type of magic *was* different. I hated keeping secrets from my friends. It didn't comport with the kind of person I wanted to be.

"Here's your chance to progress," Professor Holmes said. "If you can master the trust exercises, you'll be well on your way to graduating to the next phase of your education."

Millie's jaw was set in determination. "Fine. I volunteer." She hopped out of her seat and strode to the front of the room.

Lady Weatherby's brow lifted a fraction. "Excellent. And now you need a partner. Miss Hart, that will be you."

"Are you serious?" Millie blurted, but quickly thought better of it.

"Am I ever anything else?" Lady Weatherby asked.

I walked to the front of the class and took my place beside Millie. "What do we do?"

"Millie will use her wand first," Lady Weatherby said. "So she'll do a spell that keeps you afloat in the air as long as you believe that she can."

"And if I don't believe then I fall on the floor?" I inquired.

"Like a stone," Professor Holmes said.

I groaned. I wasn't in the market for a backache.

"This sounds like Tinker Bell coming back to life," I said. "Everyone in the audience had to believe in order for it to happen." I felt everyone's eyes on me. They had no idea what I was talking about. "Peter Pan in the theater. It's a classic."

"How interesting," Lady Weatherby said, in a tone that suggested it was not remotely interesting. "You may begin."

I stood rooted to the floor and concentrated on Millie. I

believed in her. That part was easy. Did I trust her not to drop me on the floor on purpose? Not so much.

"Emma doesn't like heights," Millie said. "What if that messes up my spell?"

"I can handle being six inches off the ground," I said. *Just don't send me much higher. I make no promises about my gag reflex.*

"The critical part of this spell is that Emma trusts you," Professor Holmes reminded her. "It's not a reflection on your ability."

Millie's shoulders relaxed and she prepared her wand. "Are you ready?"

I nodded.

This is going to be epic, Sedgwick said.

It's going to be fine, I said. *I trust her.*

Are you sure? he asked. *What about the time she made your boobs enormous with that voodoo doll?*

We resolved that.

What about all the times she made you feel like minotaur crap for not being able to ride a broom?

Stop trying to undermine me! I focused on Millie, blocking Sedgwick's voice from my thoughts.

Millie pointed her wand and spoke the same words as Professor Holmes.

I believe. I believe, I told myself. *Millie is Tinker Bell and I am the audience.*

I felt my feet slide off the floor and into the air. I wobbled slightly but remained relatively balanced as I rose higher in the air.

"She did it," Laurel said, trying to mask her disbelief.

I looked down to see Millie smiling proudly.

Sometimes it was good to believe.

CHAPTER 2

WE GATHERED in the secret lair, examining the spell in the grimoire that Laurel managed to pinch from the coven library. As remedial witches, we weren't actually permitted in the highly lauded coven library, but Laurel was so small and unassuming that she was able to slip in and out unnoticed. Who needed an invisibility spell when you were a thirteen-year-old witch who flew below the radar?

"This looks hard," Sophie complained. "It's like trying to understand a chemical equation."

"That's why I'm going to do it," Millie said, straightening her shoulders. "I'm going to show Lady Weatherby and Professor Holmes that I am more than capable of performing advanced spells."

"Your first trust exercise went well," Begonia pointed out. "That's one of the sections that tripped you up last year, but yesterday was a good start."

"I have Emma to thank for that," Millie said, surprising everyone, including me.

"I trust you, Millie," I said, despite Sedgwick's attempts to thwart that trust. "It's as simple as that."

"Of course you do. I'm very capable." Millie's nose lifted. "I can't promise the outcome would have been the same if you'd held the wand."

Heat warmed the back of my neck.

"The coven doesn't doubt your ability, Millie," Laurel said. "It's just that you don't excel in every area of witchcraft."

"No one does," Millie exploded. "And the sections I've failed aren't even important ones. It's an antiquated system and it needs to be overhauled." She pointed a finger at me. "Like your criminal punishments. You don't think those are fair so you're trying to change them."

She meant the sentencing guidelines for convicted criminals in Spellbound. "I agree with you, Millie. But it's hard to get people to make changes when they've been doing something the same way for a long time. They don't want to feel like they're wrong so they dig their heels in." I'd seen it over and over again in the human world. People willing to make situations worse only to avoid admitting an error in judgment. Not an entirely human trait apparently.

"I'm worried this will backfire," Sophie said. "Felix was a wizard, not a remedial witch." Felix was an upstart wizard who turned me invisible and then was able to make me visible again-- when he decided it was time to kill me, of course. Part of the joy in making new friends in a new town.

"Felix was a wizard, but not a particularly accomplished one," Millie reminded us. "If he can do this spell, then so can I."

I had to admire Millie's confidence. Although it often bordered on arrogance, it was a worthy trait. So many young women were prone to question themselves and look to others for approval. As annoying as Millie could be at times, I preferred her confidence to dithering.

Millie reviewed the spell on the page one more time. "There's more involved than I would've expected."

"It just shows you that Felix had planned his attack on me in advance," I said. "I knew the spell was premeditated."

"I was able to get most things on the list," Begonia said. "I had to get them from a variety of sources, though. I didn't want anyone in Mix-n-Match asking questions. Jemima was already giving me the side eye."

"Did she ask why you were buying tail of newt?" Laurel asked.

Begonia shook her head. "No, but she did make a comment when I picked up the jar of bee pollen. I told her it was for Claude. He suffers from seasonal allergies so I said it was for him."

"So you two are still a thing, huh?" Millie asked.

Begonia blushed. "He's a sweetheart. We get along well. Like old friends."

"Wish I would meet someone," Millie grumbled. "Maybe I should do a spell that makes everyone think I'm new in town. Then I could have my pick of the litter like Emma."

"You seem to forget that Emma doesn't want the pick of the litter," Sophie said. "She only has eyes for Daniel."

The mention of his name was like a dagger in my heart. The town could talk of little else besides Daniel and Elsa's upcoming nuptials. The ceremony was to be held at Swan Lake in three weeks with the reception to follow at the Spellbound Country Club. That didn't leave much time to perfect this spell and prevent the wedding from taking place.

"Well, I'm not doing this for Daniel," Millie said.

Begonia rolled her eyes. "Yes, we know Millie. You're doing this for yourself. Gods forbid you do something purely for someone else's sake."

Millie glared at her friend. "I'm here, aren't I? This isn't exactly a low risk operation. If it backfires, we can get in serious trouble."

"Even if it succeeds, we could get in serious trouble," Laurel said.

We all looked at one another, the realization settling in. We were embarking on a path that was fraught with potential landmines. Then again, it was better than watching Daniel marry someone he didn't really love. We were breaking rules, but Elsa's behavior was much worse and needed to be stopped.

"What do you think will happen to Elsa?" Sophie asked. "Do you think Mayor Knightsbridge will try to protect her?"

It was difficult to say. The mayor took her role as leader of Spellbound very seriously, but she was also a doting mother. Maybe if she hadn't doted so much on Elsa, the younger fairy wouldn't have turned into such a spoiled brat.

"I just hope the mayor doesn't take her anger out on us if we prove Elsa's guilt," Laurel said.

"The mayor is fair," Millie said. "I trust she'll do the right thing."

"For the record, I'm too young to go to prison," Laurel said.

"No one is going to prison," I said. "The worst that can happen is…"

Everyone fell silent for a moment.

"Emma could stay invisible forever and fade away," Begonia said quietly. "If we mess up, that's the worst that can happen."

I hadn't really been thinking about it that way. I'd been too focused on the potential for expulsion from the Arabella St. Simon Academy. I hadn't been thinking about the true danger involved. It didn't matter, though. Daniel's freedom was worth it to me. Even if we broke the spell and he rejected me anyway, it would still be worth it. That was how much I loved him.

"Where's the lizard saliva?" Millie asked, examining the

various bottles and jars on the coffee table. "I'm looking at the checklist and that one seems to be missing."

Laurel began to recite the list of ingredients. "One tail of newt. One fly's eye. An ounce of lizard saliva is right here." She produced a vial that had rolled behind a fat jar.

"Ew," Begonia said, scrunching up her nose. "I'm glad we don't do advanced spells. Some of these items are disgusting."

"Some?" Sophie queried. "Which ones aren't?"

"What do you want your specialty to be when you're older?" Laurel asked.

Begonia looked thoughtful. "I don't know. I keep waiting to see what I'm good at." She paused. "I'm still waiting."

I gave her arm a quick squeeze. "Begonia, you are good at so many things. That's why it's hard to choose. Not because you're not good at any."

"Like what?" Millie challenged me. "Be specific." Sometimes I really wanted to smack her, even when she was being helpful.

"Begonia is very personable," I said. "She would make a great liaison with other paranormals in town. She puts everyone at ease."

Begonia smiled. "Thanks, Emma. That means a lot coming from you."

"That's something that's missing from our classroom experience," Sophie said.

"You mean a personable head of the coven?" Millie asked. "I agree with that."

Millie was right that Lady Weatherby was not the warm and fuzzy leader that some people would prefer. She was, however, fair and smart and, when push came to shove, she supported her coven. While it was true she was a tad on the rigid side, that was probably the result of being raised by Agnes, her mother and the former free-spirited leader of the coven.

"I think it would be a great idea if we took time to focus on our strengths as individuals," I said. "Sometimes that's how you find your purpose in life. You don't always know how other people perceive you until they tell you." It was worth thinking about.

"Okay, girls," Millie said. "I think I'm ready."

My stomach clenched. The moment of truth.

"We'll give you room to work," Sophie said.

"Especially you, Sophie," Millie said. "I don't need you bumping into the coffee table and knocking all the ingredients over. We don't want to turn the whole secret lair invisible."

"I don't know," Laurel said. "That actually sounds like a good idea. It is secret after all."

We laughed. It seemed it was really the not-so-secret lair. The more witches I spoke to, the more who seemed to know about its existence. It didn't matter, though. As long as they weren't turning up and eavesdropping, it was fine. We got to keep our own space without worrying about older members of the coven supervising us.

We moved behind the sofa and watched Millie work from a safe distance.

"Shouldn't you be closer to her?" Begonia asked, nudging me.

"Not yet," Millie said, answering for me. "Let me get the spell prepped first, then I'll summon Emma over."

It sounded good to me. The door was right behind me in the event I wanted to make a last minute run for it. I knew I couldn't back down now, though. There was too much at stake. As frightened as I was to be invisible again, I trusted my friends to help if things went south.

"Light as air, thin as a breeze/Imbue this wand with the power of invisibility." Not quite a rhyme, but it didn't matter. A puff of smoke appeared above the coffee table, a hazy swirl of purple and grey. Millie waved her wand around the cloud, capturing the essence of the spell.

"Do you think it worked?" Begonia asked.

Millie peered at me over her shoulder. "Only one way to find out."

CHAPTER 3

I RODE on the broom in front of Millie. We decided it was the best way to get into town, despite my fear of heights. My only real concern was that if I fell off the broom at any point, Millie wouldn't even know it.

"If you vomit while you're invisible, will I even see it?" Millie asked. "Why did I bother asking you that? It isn't like I can hear your answer."

That was one of the downsides to the invisibility spell. No one could see me or hear me. I could, however, manipulate objects. That was how I managed to communicate last time. Good old-fashioned quill and ink.

I gripped the broom until my knuckles were taut and sore. Invisibility didn't make me any less scared to be hundreds of feet in the air on a wooden stick an inch in diameter. It didn't matter that Millie was our expert flyer. I kept my eyes closed until I felt the broom began to lower. We landed in a field of daisies not far from Elsa's house. It was an expert landing, not that I expected anything less from the star pupil of the remedial witches.

"Thanks, Millie," I said. "Even though I know you can't hear me, I appreciate what you've done today."

As though she heard me, Millie said, "Good luck, Emma. I know I don't always act like it, but I'm rooting for you."

Millie waited a couple of minutes to be on the safe side before taking off again. I stood on the edge of Elsa's neighborhood, gathering my courage. I knew from countless minutes of stalking that Elsa left the house at approximately nine o'clock two mornings a week to have her glitter done at Glow. It seemed to be a fairy thing—it was like a manicure/pedicure except they dusted your body with glitter. It seemed to be part of Elsa's regular routine rather than reserved for special occasions.

Sure enough, Elsa emerged from the house, her blond hair twisted in a French knot at the base of her neck. I cringed. Even to go to the salon, she managed to look amazing. With dark circles under my eyes and a tangle of dark hair, I usually looked like a distant relative of the trash panda.

I crept toward the house, watching for signs of Daniel. He was the uncertainty here because he didn't keep to a fixed schedule. Even if he were in the house, I'd find a way to work around him. I wasn't going to be put off by his presence. After all, I was doing this for him.

The charming house looked the same as the last time I'd been here. The front door was unlocked. Slowly and carefully, I pushed down on the handle and moved the door forward. Once the crack was big enough to see through, I surveyed the front rooms of the house. There was no sign of Daniel.

Since it was morning, Elsa would have just given him his dose of the Obsession potion before she left the house. Morning was when the obsession was at its strongest. It seemed to wane as the day went on, so I was pretty certain she had a method for topping him up throughout the day, though I wasn't sure what it was.

I squeezed through the gap in the doorway and closed it softly behind me. Walking through the house itself was easy. As long as I didn't bump into anything and knock it over, I was good. I went straight to the kitchen where I suspected she kept the potion. I'd already given a lot of thought to where she might hide it. It had to be close to the gossamer tea that she gave Daniel every morning.

I stood in front of the wide array of cabinets, trying to decide which one was the most likely. Gareth was a stickler about keeping teabags and coffee in the cabinet next to the sink. I seemed to recall that was where Elsa had taken the tea from when I'd been in the house before.

I opened the cabinet door and began rifling through the contents, careful not to make a mess. If Daniel suddenly appeared behind me, I didn't want him to see coffee filters and teabags scattered everywhere. I had no doubt that Elsa ran a tight ship.

The tea itself was easy to spot. It was right in the front and easily accessible. I was looking for a vial at the very least. The shelf was full of health tonics and beauty boosters. It was a stark contrast to my therapist's cabinet, which was only filled with booze and tonics.

A canister in the shape of a heart caught my eye. It was gaudy and seemed out of place amongst the rest of Elsa's minimalist, sleek belongings. I lifted it carefully with both hands and realized why it seemed familiar. It was made from the Mad Potter's shop, the same place Daniel took me to make the pot that sat on my mantel. I knew without a doubt this was where I would find the potion. She and Daniel had probably made this monstrosity together back when they'd dated the first time and she'd kept it all these years. Now this ugly heart housed her revenge plan. It was oddly poetic.

I removed the lid and peered inside. Jackpot. There were at least ten vials of clear liquid. As much as I wanted to, I couldn't take the entire heart canister because I couldn't let Elsa know that anyone had discovered her secret. Instead, I removed a single vial and hoped that she wouldn't notice. I slipped it into my pocket and placed the lid back on the heart. I put everything back in the cabinet exactly as I'd found it. Just as I turned to leave, Daniel padded into the kitchen. My heart stopped and my mouth became dry. His blond hair was slightly unkempt and he wore the dazed expression that I associated with Elsa's potion. I stood rooted to the floor. Even though I knew he couldn't see me, I felt paralyzed. I watched him reach for the canister of grains and oats and pour them into a bowl. His white wings were folded carefully behind him. Even tucked away, he couldn't hide their wondrous beauty. His wings were the ultimate reminder of his true nature. He was an angel, fallen or not. He deserved to have his halo restored, not simply because I loved him, but because he wanted so badly to make amends for his past transgressions. He was willing to earn it and Elsa would undoubtedly undo all of his efforts, all because of her selfishness. Daniel didn't deserve that fate. Yes, he'd wronged her once upon a time, but he'd also tried to atone for it. And even though Elsa didn't deserve to have her heart broken, she wasn't exactly an innocent. The success or failure of a relationship rested on both parties, not one.

Daniel popped a piece of bread into the toaster and raked a hand through his hair. A regretful sigh burst from my lips. Those arms. I remembered how it felt to have them wrapped around me as we danced at the Spellbound High School dance. I found myself staring at his lips and remembering how they felt brushed against mine. My pulse began to race. It had been a good kiss. Really good. The thought of never kissing him again was almost too much to endure.

I touched the vial in my pocket for reassurance and forced myself to snap out of it. Standing here lamenting what may or may not come to pass was not a productive use of my time. I had to prove Elsa's treachery and free Daniel. That was my mission and I chose to accept it.

He smeared his toast with honey, humming to himself.

"Wish me luck, Daniel," I said, moving to stand beside him. "I love you."

He bit into the toast, not a care in the world. I, on the other hand, felt like I had the weight of the world on my shoulders. I refused to fail him.

I blew him a kiss and sailed out the door.

CHAPTER 4

As I MADE my way down the front porch steps, I realized the small wrinkle in my plan. I didn't ask Millie to wait for me. Now I needed to walk all the way back to the secret lair to have the invisibility spell reversed. We should have arranged to fly back together. As much as I hated flying, my feet would have appreciated the lift, if not my stomach.

I passed through the heart of town, all too aware of the spring in my step. With the evidence on my person, I felt more confident than ever that people would believe me. More importantly, we could set to work on the Anti-Obsession potion. Once we tested the contents of the vial and confirmed its composition, then we could get right to work on the antidote. I was far more concerned with restoring Daniel to his natural state of mind than I was with punishing Elsa.

I passed Brew-Ha-Ha and briefly regretted my current state of invisibility. I wouldn't have minded a latte with a shot of 'silver linings' right now. I paused briefly at the window and peered inside to see who was there. It was still morning, so the place was heaving with customers. I saw

Britta, the deputy sheriff and Astrid's sister, sharing a table with two werewolves I didn't recognize. I took a moment to appreciate the fact that I could now recognize a werewolf on sight even in human form. I was becoming a true resident of Spellbound. Then again, maybe it was my sorceress powers kicking in. At another table sat Juliet Montlake, the Amazon who ran the bookstore and served as a member of the town council. She sat with Maeve McCullen, the banshee and fellow town council member. In the far corner of the room was Stan, the town registrar. He was deep in conversation with another elf and Donna Montrose, the new town building inspector.

As I stepped away from the window to resume my walk, the shop door opened and Markos emerged, accompanied by a young witch called Beatrice. She was probably in her late twenties. I'd seen her around at coven events, although we'd never officially met.

"I think you'd be a really good fit for the company, so just let me know when you've made your decision," Markos said.

He must have interviewed her for the available office manager role. His previous office manager recently died after trying to kill me. She'd been stealing from Markos for years and killed Ed Doyle, the town building inspector, to cover her tracks. When I got too close to the truth, she came after me as well.

"I made my decision," Beatrice said, smiling up at him. "I'm ready to start tomorrow if you'll have me."

It was the way she said 'if you'll have me' that caught my attention. It was more flirty than professional. I studied her closely and immediately recognized the glint in her eye. Beatrice had a crush on Markos. I wondered whether he saw it too. That did not bode well for a productive employer-employee relationship. The office manager shared the pent-house space with Markos. They would be working in close proximity to one another with few people around them. Not that it was any of my business. Although he'd made his interest in me very clear, I assured him that I was only interested in his friendship, especially now, so close to securing Daniel's freedom. I patted the vial in my pocket. I still didn't know what it would mean for our relationship, but it didn't matter. As long as my heart belonged to Daniel, I was incapable of giving it to anyone else.

"Great, then I'll see you tomorrow at eight o'clock sharp," Markos said. He appeared pleased and that only elevated my good mood. I wanted Markos to be happy.

I turned away and continued down the cobblestone path. I heard a happy whistling song and realized it was coming from me. The prospect of getting the real Daniel back was so close that I could taste it. I smiled broadly as I passed Wands-A-Plenty where I found Tiffany, my beloved wand. I waved to the clock tower as I passed in front of the town square. I'd grown so comfortable here. It was the home I never knew I wanted. I waved to Paws and Claws where I met Sedgwick, my cantankerous owl familiar. Then there was Ready-to-Were, the best clothing shop in town run by the most pleasant wereferret you'd ever hope to meet. With his penchant for bright colors and loud patterns, Ricardo was one of the most fashionable residents in Spellbound. I relied on him greatly whenever I needed a special outfit. I'd heard through the grapevine that Elsa had requested a wedding dress from him, but he politely declined to provide one. I wasn't sure if the rumor was true. Ultimately, it didn't matter. I was going to stop this wedding.

By the time I reached the forest, the arches of my feet were aching. I slowed my pace and tried to enjoy the tranquil scenery. The fragrant flowers. The tall, majestic trees surrounding me. They made me feel protected. Up ahead I heard the soothing sound of a babbling brook.

As I drew closer, the shrill chirping of birds began to drown out the pleasant sound of the brook. I wondered what had worked them into a frenzy. Maybe a dead animal had upset them. I grimaced. I wasn't eager to see the carcass of a fox or a rabbit.

It didn't take me long to figure out what the birds were so worked up about. On the ground was a figure about three feet in length. Had a child gotten lost in the woods and been hurt? I sprinted to the body and the birds scattered.

"Are you okay?" I asked.

I dropped to my knees beside the body and quickly saw that it was a troll, not a child, and he was definitely not okay. His eyes and mouth were wide open, as though shocked by his own fate. When I touched his arm, I realized that he was frozen solid. I reached for my wand but remembered that I didn't have it. Not that it would have done the troll any good. I was fairly certain he was dead.

I touched his leg and his head. Everywhere on his body was completely frozen. Had he been out here all night? Even if he had, it was unlikely he would have frozen to death. The temperature in Spellbound never fell that low. I sighed. If it wasn't due to natural causes, then we likely had another murder on our hands. I glanced around the forest. There was no one in sight. Who knew how long the troll had been here? I debated returning to town and finding Astrid, but it would be difficult in my invisible form. I would need to hurry back to the secret lair and tell the other witches. I hated to leave the troll like this, but it was the best option. The girls could turn me visible again and fly back to the sheriff's office to tell Astrid where to find the troll's body. I couldn't even close his eyes out of respect because his eyelids were frozen open. Poor troll. I glanced at the bridge over the brook and wondered whether he had been hiding there. I knew it was a violation of the town ordinance for trolls to reside under bridges, but I also knew that not all residents were following the ordinances. More and more, it seemed that residents were starting small rebellions. If it was in a troll's nature to live under a bridge, then I could understand the resistance.

I stood and placed my hands on my hips, contemplating the troll. It was best not to move him at all. I took a deep breath and began to run. I raced across the bridge and through the forest until the trees grew few and far between. Once the trees disappeared all together, I knew I was nearly at the foothills where the secret lair was located. Periodically I checked my pocket to make sure the vial was safe. I couldn't risk losing the one piece of evidence in my possession.

When I reached the hidden door of the lair, I realized that I wouldn't be able to get in the usual way. I could place my hand on the stone, but because my hand was invisible, the stone didn't register my palm print. I chuckled to myself. Not quite the foolproof plan I thought it was.

"Hello," I shouted, knowing perfectly well that no one could hear me. I looked around for a decent sized stone and threw it at the exterior of the lair. I repeated this multiple times until, to my relief, the secret door opened to reveal Millie.

"I'm going to assume that's you Emma," she snapped. "Just come in and don't throw any more stones. I don't feel like being knocked unconscious."

I hurried inside and placed the vial on the coffee table. The other witches gasped.

"I can't believe it," Sophie said, nearly breathless.

"We should never have doubted you, Emma," Begonia said.

No, they shouldn't have, but I didn't blame them. It didn't surprise me that they felt my feelings for Daniel colored my view of the situation. I completely understood.

Millie lifted the grimoire from the coffee table and

flipped to the appropriate page. "We're ready and waiting for you. I prepared the spell while you were gone."

Good thinking.

Millie folded her arms. "I suppose you'd like to be visible again."

Begonia elbowed Millie in the ribs. "Of course she would. Now do it already and stop dragging this out."

Millie narrowed her eyes at Begonia. "You're not the boss of me, Begonia Spence." She retrieved her wand and glanced around the room. "Stand right here in front of me. I put the spell on my wand again so I need to tap you. I'll count to three."

I did as I was told and waited for Millie to count. She reached three and tapped the top of my head.

A gust of cold wind blew through the cave and I knew I was visible again.

"Spell's bells, Emma," Millie said. "Your hair is a mess."

"Millie, you did it," Laurel exclaimed.

Millie smiled, pleased with her achievement.

I threw my arms around her. "Thank you, Millie," I said. "You have no idea what this means to me."

"I hope Lady Weatherby is as appreciative as you are," Millie said. "I'd really like to graduate from the remedial program this year." I knew it was a bone of contention for Millie that she was still there. In truth, she was a much better witch than the rest of us. Of course, the fact that I wasn't actually a witch was a factor. Not that the others needed to know about my true identity. Daniel and I had made a pact to keep the news to ourselves for my safety and the comfort of the rest of Spellbound.

"So what now?" Laurel asked. "I suppose we need to confirm what's in that vial."

I looked at Sophie. "Do you think your mother will do it?" Sophie's mother was a master mixologist in the coven. If anyone could break down the components of the potion, she could. It was a bonus that we trusted her.

"Absolutely," Sophie said. "Mom will be happy to help."

I examined the vial in my hand. "You know what? Let me show this to Mayor Knightsbridge first as proof of Elsa's wrongdoing and then I'll send it over to your mother. If I can get the mayor on board, we may not even need to make our own Anti-Obsession potion."

Laurel looked skeptical. "You think the mayor will make Elsa stop giving him the potion?"

"She doesn't want to see them married either," I said. "She didn't believe that Elsa would stoop to magic to win Daniel, but she'll have to believe me now."

"I guess that's your next stop then," Sophie said.

My hand flew to cover my mouth. "Stars and stones. Not quite. We need to get a message to Astrid." I explained what happened in the forest with the troll. I was so caught up in the wedding mess that I forgot all about the poor troll.

"You think he was murdered?" Millie asked.

I shrugged. "I'm not sure, but it seems unlikely that it was natural causes."

"It could have been an accident," Begonia said hopefully.

"Yes, of course. I'll let the experts make that determination."

"I have my owl with me," Begonia said. "We can send a note to Astrid. Just tell me the location of the troll."

"Good idea, thanks."

While Begonia scribbled a message with the location of the troll's body, Sophie decided to accompany Laurel back to the coven library so that she could return the grimoire unnoticed.

"What are you going to do now?" Millie asked.

"I'm going to meet Astrid in the forest and see if I can be of any help," I said.

"Really?" Millie asked, quirking an eyebrow. "I would've expected you to be making a beeline for the mayor."

"I will, as soon as I finish with Astrid."

"But a dead troll has nothing to do with you," Millie countered. "The spell on Daniel is the priority. That affects you directly."

"If there's one thing I've learned from living in a small town, it's that everything that happens affects everyone. Maybe we'll only feel the effect in tiny ripples instead of waves, but we'll feel it. And, yes, Daniel is my priority, but the troll was a member of this community and we owe it to him to figure out what happened. An extra half an hour before I speak to the mayor isn't going to make a difference. It's not like the wedding is today."

Millie's cheeks reddened. "I guess I never thought about it that way before."

"There's a saying in the human world—'it takes a village.'"

Millie's face lit up. "Yes, we say 'it takes a coven.'"

"But that mindset is part of the problem right there," I said. "It doesn't just take a coven. It takes everyone in the town. We all matter. Every single one of us."

Millie stared at me, the words sinking in. "So do you need a ride back to the forest?"

CHAPTER 5

IT WASN'T AS easy to land between the trees as it was to land in an open field, but Millie handled it with aplomb. Thanks to a healthy dose of anti-anxiety potion that morning, I managed to endure a second ride without spilling my guts. Literally.

The second my feet touched the ground, I was off the broom. I always felt better when I was attached to the earth. Gravity was my friend.

"Boy, you weren't kidding," Millie said, moving closer to examine the troll. "The stiff is truly stiff."

"I told you," I said. "Do you know of a spell that freezes people?"

Millie gave a dismissive flick of her fingers. "There are dozens. I can think of several right off the top of my head."

"Are they easy to perform?" I asked. "Maybe it's something that a non-magic user could look up in the library and do successfully."

Millie frowned. "It's possible, I suppose. I really don't know. Most spells come so easily to me. It's hard to gauge whether these would be easy or difficult for anyone else."

The sound of footsteps alerted us to Astrid and Britta's arrival. The Valkyrie sisters smiled when they saw me.

"Emma Hart, we have to stop meeting like this," Astrid said.

"You got my message?" I asked.

"Well, it wasn't Sedgwick delivering the message, but as soon as I saw the words 'dead body,' I knew you were somehow involved," Astrid said.

"I'm worried that I'm beginning to develop a reputation," I joked.

Astrid kneeled beside the body. "Yep. He's dead all right."

"Are you sure he's not mostly dead?" I asked.

"That's a reference to something I don't get, right?" Astrid asked.

I dug my toe in the dirt. "*The Princess Bride*," I mumbled.

Britta began scanning the area around the bridge.

"Anything of interest over there?" Astrid asked.

Britta shook her head. "Not yet, but I want to give it a good, thorough once-over."

"Look for footprints in and out of the area," Astrid advised her. "I can see where the body was dragged a little." She pointed to marks leading away from his shoulders.

"So he may not have died in this spot," I said. Interesting. Was it possible someone went to a lot of trouble to leave him where he would be difficult to find?

"Hard to tell," Astrid said.

"How busy is this section of the forest?" I asked. I only came this way because I was going to the secret lair in the foothills. I wasn't sure why anyone else would use this particular path.

"I don't see many footprints," Britta confirmed. "I imagine these two sets belong to you and your friend."

"Millie," Millie said. It seemed to rankle her that Britta didn't know her name.

"Sorry, Millie," Britta said. "I meet a lot of witches."

Millie put a hand on her hip. "And what? We all look alike? Is that what you're trying to say?"

Britta bit back a smile. "Not at all. It just means my memory sucks."

"I find it ironic that someone descended from a small pool of blond, blue-eyed Vikings would comment on the indistinguishable nature of witches. At least we have varying hair and eye colors."

Astrid positioned herself between Britta and Millie. "My sister sometimes speaks without thinking. Chill. She wasn't trying to insult you."

Millie backed down, although I could tell she was still annoyed. Not that that was anything new for Millie. She seemed annoyed when the wind blew in the 'wrong' direction.

"Hmm," Astrid said. "Whatever froze the troll seems to have killed this flower too."

I peered over her shoulder to see a dead flower on the ground. "What makes you think so?"

Astrid touched it. "The petals are wet. Like it had been frozen to death and then thawed."

Weird.

"Let's get this body to the lab," Astrid said. "Maybe there's a slim chance we can thaw him out like the flower."

"But the flower's dead," Britta reminded her.

"Will you let me know when you have an ID?" I asked.

"Sure," Astrid said.

"You're doing a great job, by the way. Everyone in town seems to respect you." That was so important after enduring Sheriff Hugo's reign.

"Thank you," Astrid said, beaming. "That means a lot. I appreciate the vote of confidence."

"Like I said, let me know if you need help with the case," I said.

"Don't you have a case of your own to handle?" Britta asked. For a brief moment, I thought she meant the situation with Daniel, but I quickly realized that she meant my role as public defender.

"Not yet," I said. "But with Spellbound's love of rules and regulations, there's sure to be one tomorrow."

I hitched a ride with Astrid and Britta back into town and walked the rest of the way to the Mayor's Mansion. I didn't want to push my luck on Millie's broom. Twice in one day seemed more than enough.

I took the steps two at a time and pounded on the over-sized door. I steadied my breathing. I needed to remain calm when I spoke with the mayor. Even though she didn't want this marriage to happen either, Elsa was still her daughter. I couldn't rush in with guns blazing.

The door opened to reveal the mayor's right hand and my good friend, Lucy.

"Hey, Lucy. I'd like to speak with the mayor, please," I said, struggling to maintain a calm exterior.

Lucy grimaced. "Oh no! Who died this time?" she asked.

Okay, so not such a hot job with the whole calm exterior part. "Nobody died." I hesitated, realizing my mistake. "Well, actually someone did die. A troll, but that's not why I'm here."

Lucy frowned. "A troll died? Who?"

"Not sure yet. He needs to be identified."

Lucy assessed me. "If you're not here about the troll, then what's the emergency?"

I paused. I couldn't burden her with this information. I had to speak with the mayor first. "Lucy, you're a good friend, but this is a private matter between the mayor and me."

She narrowed her eyes. "You two seem to have had a few private matters recently. Care to share?"

"I wish I could." I really did. I hated hiding things from my friends.

Lucy consulted her planner. "Well, the mayor's hosting a fairy tea party right now. Can it wait until, say, five o'clock?"

"A fairy tea party?" I queried.

"She hosts a monthly event with a different paranormal group in town. Last month was a werewolf barbecue." She paused. "I don't mean we cooked the werewolves. We fed them. This month is a fairy tea party."

I craned my neck to see down the long hall all the way to the back patio. I saw streamers in a rainbow of pastel colors and lots of white serving dishes. "Looks like a nice event."

Lucy flapped her pink wings. "She does tend to throw in a little extra pizazz for our kind. So come back at five?"

"No, sorry. This can't wait until five."

Lucy chewed her lip. "Okay, fine. Go ahead, but as far as the mayor's concerned, I never saw you. You breezed right in while I was in the bathroom."

"Works for me."

Lucy fluttered into a front room and I headed straight to the back patio. There were roughly thirty fairies fluttering around the back of the mansion. It was a lovely day for a tea party. The air was pleasantly warm and, more importantly, perfectly still so that napkins and streamers weren't blowing around and the fairies' skirts stayed put. The mayor stood by the cookie table, in the middle of a conversation with a trio of fairies I didn't recognize. Her lips pursed ever so slightly when she saw me.

"Emma Hart, what a pleasant surprise. Who would have expected a witch to turn up at the fairy tea party?" She beckoned me over. "Have you met my dear friends, Cindy and Ken Applewhite and their daughter, Anya?"

Anya was a carbon copy of her mother. They both had white blond hair and distinctive grey eyes. Their wings were a soft lavender that I'd never seen before. With his dark hair and dark eyes, Ken Applewhite appeared more shifter than fairy, but his orange wings gave him away.

"Nice to meet you," I said. "Do you go to Spellbound High School?" And, if so, why wasn't she there now in the middle of a school day?

Anya lowered her gaze. "I go to the Fairy Charter School. At least I did."

Ken cleared his throat. "Anya's taking some time off."

From the expression on Anya's face, it appeared that the time off was involuntary.

"She's not badly behaved or anything," Cindy blurted. "She just needs to hone her craft. Not everyone excels in a classroom setting."

I felt an immediate pang of sympathy. So Anya was a remedial fairy.

"That's so true, Mrs. Applewhite," I said. "I know a few amazing witches who can't necessarily perform on command in a classroom, but they're smart and very capable."

Anya beamed at me. "Really?"

I nodded. "Absolutely. I also knew plenty of people in the human world who didn't do well in school, but they still managed to find their niche in life later on."

"I don't want to learn fairy magic," Anya confessed. "It's boring and I'm not good at it."

"Thank you for the pep talk," the mayor interrupted, clearly annoyed by the conversation. "I take it there's a reason for this unscheduled visit."

"Yes, Madame Mayor. There certainly is. Could I steal you away for a few minutes?" I asked.

"Of course." Although she smiled, her eyes formed dangerous slits. "Why don't we step into my office? Excuse us, please. Try the cucumber and basil muffins. They're divine."

As soon as we crossed the threshold into the house, the mayor glared at me. "You'd better have a good reason for crashing the fairy tea party. I take these events very seriously."

"Trust me. It's a good reason."

We entered the office and she closed the door behind us. She didn't bother to sit behind her desk like she usually did.

"Out with it," she demanded, fluttering in front of me.

"I told you I thought Elsa was using an Obsession potion on Daniel."

She rolled her eyes. "Yes, I recall that you shared your absurd theory with me."

"Right. Well, now I have proof." I produced the vial of potion from my pocket. "I took this from her kitchen cabinet."

Mayor Knightsbridge stiffened and the color drained from her face. "So you claim. You could have concocted that yourself, dear."

"It was hidden in a ceramic canister. The ugly heart one. She keeps it on the shelf above the tea."

The mayor's eyes rounded just enough that I knew she understood. This was real. This was the truth.

"And how did you manage to obtain this evidence?" she asked. "I don't suppose my daughter willingly handed it over."

"I took it when she wasn't home," I said, leaving out the invisibility spell. We'd save that part of the story to impress Lady Weatherby.

"And what do you intend to do with this information?" she asked, examining me.

"I intend to give Daniel an Anti-Obsession potion to counteract it."

She arched an eyebrow. "And what about Elsa?"

"You're the mayor and on the town council. What do you think should happen to Elsa?"

"How should I know? I'm also her devoted mother." Mayor Knightsbridge sighed and flew around the room, thinking. "She's my only child. I owe it to her to protect her. You'll understand that one day when you have children of your own."

If I had children of my own. I'd learned the hard way that there were no guarantees in life.

"What Elsa did was wrong," I said. "She was manipulating Daniel's feelings with magic."

The mayor waved a dismissive hand. "And how is that any different from manipulating a man with clothes that hide your flaws or offer imaginary enhancements like a push-up bra? Or using sex, for that matter?"

"Because the potion is different. It makes him feel a way he doesn't actually feel," I said, my cheeks flushed with anger. "Those pretend feelings have consequences, not just for Daniel and Elsa, but for other innocent people like Jasper."

The mayor gave me a pointed look. "And like you?"

"Of course like me," I shot back. "You don't even like Daniel. I would think this is happy news for you. Now we can stop the wedding once and for all."

"But at what cost?" the mayor asked. "I won't have my Elsa's reputation tarnished. We must preserve the good Knightsbridge name."

"I don't see how we can get around that," I said. "She committed a despicable act. She needs to be held accountable."

The mayor's large blue wings stopped fluttering and her

feet dropped gracefully to the floor. "What if I made a deal with you?"

My conscience was on high alert. "What kind of deal?"

"You've been wanting to create this committee to revise the sentencing guidelines, correct? You think the Spellbound laws are too harsh on its citizens."

I swallowed hard. I already knew where she was going and I didn't like it. Not one bit.

"Yes. You know as well as anyone that the sentencing in Spellbound tends to be too rigid. The prison time assigned to certain crimes is far longer than necessary. I advocate a more flexible approach."

She smiled. "Very well. I'll fast track approval for the committee at the next town council meeting. You can organize your team by the end of next week if you wish."

"In exchange for my silence about Elsa?"

"Yes. And Daniel still gets his freedom, of course."

I stood frozen in front of the mayor. A reformation of the sentencing guidelines would benefit the entire community. All I needed to do was stay quiet about one selfish fairy. Her punishment was never my top priority, however, I didn't love the idea that she'd get away unscathed.

I lifted my chin a fraction. "And what if I don't agree?"

"Then perhaps your committee will never get off the ground." She pretended to examine her bright pink fingernails. "A shame. Your idea showed real promise. A huge benefit to so many in the town."

I closed my eyes and took a deep breath, trying to clear my head. Surely the needs of many trumped the need to punish one fairy. I hoped Daniel forgave me for striking this deal since he was the one who deserved a voice in Elsa's punishment.

"If we do it your way, what are the terms?" I asked. The words tasted like acid on my tongue.

"What we just discussed, plus you'll need to use your feminine wiles to make sure Mr. Starr agrees to the terms, once he's back to his usual mental state, of course. The gods know he's caused me enough grief for one lifetime." She snapped her fingers. "And I'll have the vial, dear. Can't risk you changing your mind and using it against my Elsa."

"I need it to create the Anti-Obsession potion," I objected.

"Not anymore," the mayor said. "I'll handle it from here. It may take a few days to sort out, so do try to exercise patience, dear."

"What will you say to Elsa to make her hand over the rest of the vials?"

"How I handle my daughter is my business," she said. "Now give me the vial so I can return to my guests." She wiggled her fingers. "Are you making this deal, Emma? Because I'm about to flutter out the door."

I placed the vial in her petite palm. "Yes, Mayor Knightsbridge, I'm making the deal." With the devil in a pink dress, apparently, but a deal nonetheless.

CHAPTER 6

APPARENTLY THE CRIMINAL gods were listening to Britta because a case landed in my lap the very next day. I dropped by to make sure Althea hadn't turned my office into a distillery during my absence. Thankfully, the vat of moonshine was gone and the plants on the windowsill were looking spry and healthy.

"Oh good," Althea said. "I wasn't sure if I would see you today. You have a client coming in at two o'clock."

I stared at her. "So if I hadn't come in today, then what would've happened? Would you have sent the client to my house?"

Althea shrugged. "Who knows? It hasn't happened yet. It's like you have a sixth sense for these things."

Her snakes hissed in solidarity.

"Your latte smells good," I said, sniffing the rich aroma.

"Is that a hint? I don't do passive-aggressive. If you want one, you only need to ask."

I gave her a sheepish grin. "Only if you're not too busy. I don't want to interrupt your work." Whatever work she could possibly have without me, I had no idea, but she always seemed occupied.

She waved me off. "These legs are always looking for an excuse to take a walk. Sitting behind a desk all day isn't good for anyone and I need to keep my girls happy." She patted her headscarf. "They like the sun."

I shared the sentiment. Winters in Lemon Grove, Pennsylvania were long and hard. There were times when one more day with a grey sky would have ended me.

"The weather is one of the things I love about Spellbound," I said. "No one here will ever suffer from seasonal affective disorder."

"I've been meaning to ask you," Althea said. "How's therapy going? Or should I not ask?"

"No, it's fine to ask." After all, Althea was the one who suggested it. "Dr. Hall is… interesting."

Althea laughed. "That's one way of describing her. She's a character, I agree. She told you the story about the Kraken, I take it?"

I nodded. "One of many stories. She seems to have an endless supply."

"Of stories and booze. I heard she does shots during session," Althea said with an air of disapproval.

"I can neither confirm nor deny this," I said. Dr. Hall's methods were unorthodox, but if she was helping people then I had no problem with it. "That reminds me—do you know anything about her relationship with Lord Gilder?" Althea had been around long enough to know the gossip.

Althea pursed her lips. "I do remember hearing rumblings of a connection. That was a long time ago though. I don't know that anything became of it. Why?"

"I just think maybe that ship hasn't sailed," I said. "Not for her anyway."

"Is that so?" Althea asked. "Interesting. As far as I know, Lord Gilder hasn't been seen with anyone in a good, long while. He's a lovely vampire. It would be nice to see him happy."

"I could say the same for you," I said. "Aren't you interested in meeting anyone?"

"Girl, when you've been around as long as I have, you're grateful for a couple of decades of solitude. I'll get back in there eventually. Time to oneself is underrated."

"You're saying there were no great romances in your past? No one who made you lose yourself completely?"

"I didn't say that," Althea replied. She drew a breath. "There was one man. A human, in fact."

"Really?"

"Which surprises you more?" she asked. "That I was in love or that he was human?"

"The human part," I said truthfully.

Her dark eyes took on a dreamy quality. "His name was Percy and he was the most wonderful man I'd ever met. Kind and generous. Smart and funny."

"What happened?" I asked.

Her eyes rolled upward. "I couldn't risk turning him to stone."

"So you keep them covered," I said. "There's no risk, right?"

"You don't understand," Althea said. "We were crazy for each other. We couldn't be in the same room without undressing."

Color blossomed on my cheeks. Not the answer I was expecting.

"We'd be in such a state of passion, we'd hardly notice when my headscarf began to slide off." She touched her head absently. "We had too many near misses. It became dangerous for him to see me."

"There was nothing you could do?" I asked. "No spell to keep him from turning to stone?"

"Not then," Althea said. "Maybe now I could find someone..." She glanced away. "It doesn't matter. This was a long time ago and he isn't here."

And if he were human, he would have died many years ago. "I'm sorry, Althea. That's so sad."

"Better to have loved and lost than to have never loved at all," she said with a shrug. "I have many happy memories of our time together. They keep me warm on many a night."

"I hope someday you meet another Percy," I said.

"There was only one Percy in the world, but I hope to find love again. Just not this decade."

I didn't argue. Althea seemed content with her situation. That was fine by me. It was people like Dr. Hall who seemed stuck in a situation they'd rather not be in. She was someone I felt inclined to help.

"Dr. Hall needs love this decade," I said. "And so does Lord Gilder."

Althea gave me a curious look. "Now don't go sticking your nose in where it doesn't belong, Nancy Drew."

"I don't think Nancy Drew dabbled in romances," I said. "Nice attempt at a human world reference, though."

Althea folded her arms across her chest. "You know exactly what I'm saying Little Mary Sunshine. Let me get you that latte before your meeting."

"And the file would be great too," I called after her. She slammed the door behind her and I laughed.

I didn't manage to get the file before my client arrived. The second he swaggered through the door, I knew I was dealing with a werewolf. If his brown hair and brown eyes weren't a giveaway, then his natural masculinity would have tripped the werewolf alarm. He stood in front of my desk and stared down at me like I was prime rib with the bone in and he couldn't wait to suck the marrow out of me.

"You must be my two o'clock," I said, inching my chair back slightly. He seemed like he might reach across the desk and grab me by the back of the hair. He was definitely giving off a caveman vibe. Not that I was painting all werewolves with the same testosterone brush. Alex Ramon, the rising pack leader, was masculine without being obnoxious. I met him after the death of his fiancée and respected him greatly. I also knew if I had any trouble with a werewolf that I could go to Alex or Lorenzo Mancini, although Lorenzo was decidedly less fond of me.

"Two o'clock? I'm your anytime you want," he said with a wink.

I groaned. "Have a seat. What's your name?"

He dropped into the chair, his legs spread wide. Manspread. I had a direct line of sight to his crotch and it wasn't a view I was interested in.

"Buck," he said. "Buck Testani."

"Nice to meet you, Buck," I said. "Why don't you tell me about your case?" I silently cursed Althea for not giving me time to prepare. Not that I would ever curse her out loud. I wasn't an idiot.

"I think they call it an indecent exposure charge," he said, scratching his beard. "I'm pretty sure that's what the sheriff said when she clicked the cuffs on me. Two blond sisters restraining me..." He whistled. "Now that's a man's dream."

I cringed inwardly. Indecent exposure? Oh dear.

"Would you mind expanding on that?" In this town, there was never a dull moment.

He leered at me. "I'd love to expand on that," he said, in a way that suggested he was making a sexual euphemism.

Unfortunately, I couldn't quite work out what the euphemism was.

"Where did this happen?" I asked.

"The bottom half," he said, gesturing to his crotch. "No one's going to object to the top half. My pecs are outstanding."

"Not where on your body," I huffed. "Where as in the location in town?"

"Oh." He didn't seem the least bit embarrassed. "Near the Oaks, on the border of the siren's yard."

"Which siren?"

"I think her name is Alison. She sings. Got a real nice voice. I heard her through the open window before she caught me." He hesitated. "Her voice wasn't so nice after that. Man, she can really screech. A pitch only wolves can hear."

I didn't blame her. "So you flashed her? Is that something you do often?" If I was dealing with a pervert, I needed to know now. I'd be sure to have Althea sit in on every meeting with Buck.

"Flashed her? What does that mean? No, I pissed on her lawn in my wolf form. She saw me and freaked out. I turned back into my human form so I could talk to her, but when she saw me naked, she freaked out even more." He pounded his chest. "I mean, would you freak out if you saw this fine specimen on your front lawn? You'd be kissing the ground and thanking the gods that your prayers had been answered."

I resisted the urge to groan loudly. So Buck fancied himself the gods' gift to women. Go figure.

"Now Buck," I said. "I'm sure you're aware of the ordinances that disallow urination on someone else's property." Not that an ordinance should be necessary for that one. Common sense would do, too. "Furthermore, I'm sure you're aware of the shifting ordinances that are currently in place. It sounds to me like you violated two of those, if not more."

He grinned. "You should've seen the look on her face. She was not expecting me to shift to human form."

I pressed my fingers to my temples. "Buck, in some circles, what you did could also be viewed as sexual harassment. Alison is a single woman who lives alone. She probably felt threatened by the presence of a naked man on her front lawn. Did you ever consider that? I bet you really frightened her."

"I wasn't there to scare her," he said. "I needed to take a leak and her lawn was there. Her singing was so nice, I stopped to listen. I didn't expect her to come running at me like a crazy person."

"Be that as it may, you are now sitting here with me, facing criminal charges. Do you know what the punishment is for your particular violations?"

His expression clouded over. "No. Am I looking at jail time?"

I sighed. "To be honest, I don't know. I'm unprepared for this meeting, but I'll find out the details. Why don't we set up another meeting for Friday?"

His eyes sparkled. "How about Friday night? We can talk over dinner at Alessandro's."

"We'll talk in my office in the daytime," I said. "And I would advise you to use the bathroom before you leave the house. No pit stops."

He laughed and slapped his leg. "You're funny. I like a funny girl."

I glared at him. "Buck, this funny girl wants to keep you out of prison." Maybe. Right now I wasn't so sure.

He made an obnoxious clicking sound. "Because I'm too hot for prison, right?"

My head drooped. "Yes, Buck. Because you're too hot for prison. See you on Friday."

CHAPTER 7

THE DEAD TROLL was identified as Walter Rivers. Even if the team hadn't been able to identify him, his frantic wife would have been a tipoff.

I knew Astrid and Britta were still waiting for the medical examiner to finish with the body, so I decided to stop by Brew-Ha-Ha and grabbed them a couple of lattes to enjoy while they waited.

"You are the best assistant I never had," Britta said, greedily accepting the calm-infused latte. I'd given Astrid's a shot of authority.

"I thought you both could use a nice, warm drink while you waited," I said.

"Thanks," Astrid said. "Too bad our victim can't use this to thaw out."

"It wasn't possible to use a counterspell to thaw him out?" I asked.

"It was too late for this guy. In any case, it depends on the type of magic used," Astrid said. "It's hard to do a counterspell if you're not countering the right one."

Like the Anti-Obsession potion. "Then what's the

alternative?"

Britta gulped down her latte. "Good, old-fashioned science. The medical examiner has heat lamps generated by magical energy. They stay on him until his body temperature returns to normal."

Well, as normal as possible for a corpse.

"His blood is probably going to give the most information," Astrid said. "We need it in liquid form, though."

At that moment, the doors burst open and a stout woman came flying into the room, her clothes askew and her hair sticking out in all directions.

"Sheriff Astrid," the woman said. She looked from Astrid to Britta, slightly confused. "Okay, you're both Valkyries. Which one of you is the sheriff?"

Astrid raised her hand. "You're looking at her."

"Thank goodness. I thought I might need a new eye prescription. My name is Marianne Rivers," the woman said. "My husband is missing. I've looked in all the usual places, but I don't know what else to do."

Of course. Marianne Rivers was obviously a troll. With her stout body and wide nose, it should have been obvious to me, even without my newer, finely honed instincts.

"What's your husband's name, Mrs. Rivers?" Astrid asked, feigning ignorance.

"Walter," she said, wringing her hands anxiously. "He went out for an early morning walk yesterday and I haven't seen him since. I'm worried that he might have fallen and be stuck somewhere. I need help."

"You haven't seen him since yesterday morning but you're only reporting it now?" Astrid queried.

Marianne blushed. "My husband's an inventor. It's not unusual for him to stay overnight if he's close to a break-through on a project."

"Was he unwell?" Astrid asked. "Is there a reason you believe he might have fallen?"

"Oh no," Marianne said. "I just couldn't think of any other reason why he still hasn't come home. I tried to walk along the path near the house and retrace his steps, but I honestly don't know his usual route. He always walks alone in the mornings. I assumed he went to work afterward, but apparently he didn't."

"He walks every morning?" I asked. "This is part of his usual routine?" If someone had targeted him, then they would know that he walked at the same time every morning.

Marianne pressed her plump lips together. "Yes. Most days. It was his thinking time before work."

Astrid came out from behind the desk and placed an arm around Marianne's shoulders. "Mrs. Rivers, would you mind coming with me into my private office? There's something I need to tell you."

Marianne shook off Astrid's hand. "Whatever it is, you can tell me right here. I'm a troll. You don't need to sugarcoat it for me."

Astrid hesitated. I could tell she hated to be the harbinger of bad news. Unfortunately, that was part and parcel of the job.

"Mrs. Rivers, I'm afraid that your husband is dead. We found him yesterday near Larkspur Bridge. He was frozen to death."

Marianne's round eyes grew even rounder. "Dead?" she repeated. "I don't understand. How can he be dead? He was perfectly healthy."

"The fact that he was in a frozen state suggests murder," Astrid said. "We're trying to get more information on the spell that might have been used so that we can narrow down the suspects. Is there anyone you can think of that may have had a grudge against your husband?"

Tears streamed down Marianne's cheeks. She didn't bother to wipe them away. "No. No. Everyone loves Walter. He made friends wherever we went. If he asked to hold your baby at the parade and you'd let him."

A warm and fuzzy troll. "Where did he work?" I asked. Maybe there was a problem at the office that his wife was unaware of. Not everyone shared professional problems with a spouse.

"Walter was a mechanic at Quinty's. He's worked there for many years. I can't imagine there was any problem."

"A mechanic?" Britta repeated. "You said he worked on inventions."

"He did both," Marianne said. "Mechanic paid the bills but inventing was his passion."

"Quinty," I repeated. "He's the elf that converted my regular car into a magical one."

Marianne smiled. "Quinty is a talented inventor. He and Walter worked together on a lot of those special projects. I try not to be envious of the hours he's spent bent over some magical engine. The worst is when he doesn't call to tell me he's going to be late. He gets so wrapped up in a project that dinner will be cold by the time he arrives. Always makes me feel guilty."

I gave her a sympathetic smile. "At least it sounds like Walter really enjoyed his work. Not everyone is so fortunate."

Marianne nodded and Britta handed her a tissue to wipe away the flood of tears that followed.

"What about a problem with any neighbors?" Astrid asked. "Any border disputes? A problem with a customer?"

Marianne dabbed at her eyes. "Nothing that he told me about. Walter was a very upbeat guy for a troll. He didn't have that grumpy gene that so many of us seem to carry. It's one of the things I really appreciate about him."

Walter sounded like a wonderful troll. It was too bad.

"Do you have any children, Mrs. Rivers?" I asked. Sometimes children had more insight into a parent's moods or activities. I could've given someone an earful about my grandparents' relationship growing up. Things I was sure they'd never noticed about each other. As a child, I was the silent observer in the house.

Mrs. Rivers began to cry in earnest. "No children. We wanted them, but it never happened. It was a shame because Walter would've made a brilliant father. So much joy and love to give."

My heart ached for her. Mrs. Rivers had a long road to recovery ahead. I didn't envy her.

"If you think of anything else, Mrs. Rivers," Astrid said, "please don't hesitate to send me a message or stop by."

Mrs. Rivers sniffed. "I will. You'll keep me informed, won't you? I need to know what happened to my Walter."

Astrid patted her on the back. "My goal is to give you closure, Mrs. Rivers."

"Would you like me to walk you home?" I asked. "Or maybe call a friend to come and get you?"

"That's very kind of you," Marianne said. "I'm happy to walk. I'll need the time to clear my head. How ironic. Walter was always trying to get me to exercise more. He'll be laughing if he can see me now."

I doubted that very much. If Walter was half the troll his wife believed, then he was very sad right now.

We watched Mrs. Rivers leave the office, her body language far less energetic than when she entered.

"At least we can get started now," Astrid said. "While we're waiting for more information from the lab, we can pay a visit to Quinty."

"Quinty is awesome," Britta said. "He'll be a good source of information."

"About that…" Astrid hesitated. "You two are friends."

"So what?" Britta replied.

Astrid eyed her sister. "In that case, you should probably sit this one out."

Britta's expression slackened. "Sit this one out? No way."

"I don't mean the whole investigation," Astrid assured her. "I just mean the interview with Quinty. I don't want your relationship to color the questioning."

"Fair enough," Britta grumbled. "I'll hold down the fort here. If the medical examiner comes up with anything, I'll let you know."

Astrid gave her sister a gentle punch in the arm. "Thanks, sis." She turned to me. "How about you, counselor? Got any plans today?"

My plans involved keeping myself distracted until Daniel showed up at my door, clear-eyed and back to his normal self. I imagined him shaking off the potion this very moment.

I smiled. "I'd love to meet the elf who transformed Sigmund into a magical machine. Lead on."

CHAPTER 8

QUINTY'S WORKSHOP was located along the same route as the church and the Shamrock Casino. It was still close to town, but far enough from the tightknit buildings to have space for his various warehouses and inventions. I was expecting more of a traditional auto body, so I was surprised to see something more akin to Thomas Edison's house. I'd visited there as a child with my grandparents. My grandfather had been a real fan of Edison's. I remembered thinking the trip would be boring, but was surprised to find how much I'd enjoyed it. I also recalled being amazed by Edison's work schedule. He napped periodically throughout the day. The ultimate power napper.

We stepped inside the main office where we were greeted by an elf behind the desk. Her slight frame was adorned in a yellow sundress, revealing pale, narrow shoulders. Her light brown hair hung loose in the back but was pinned up on the sides, revealing her pointed ears.

"Good afternoon, Sheriff," she said. "Are you here for a repair?"

"No. I'd like to speak to Quinty," she said.

The elf's brow lifted slightly. "Is there a problem?"

"Have you noticed anyone missing from work today?" Astrid asked.

The elf looked thoughtful. "Not that I can think of. Bernard called out sick and it's Walter's day off."

Sadly, all of Walter's days were off now.

"We'd like to see Quinty, if that's at all possible," Astrid said firmly.

The elf pushed back her chair and nodded. She scurried to a far corner of the office and opened the door without knocking.

"Pansy," a voice cried. "You know better than to interrupt me when I'm in the middle of something."

Astrid and I exchanged looks. A temperamental inventor. I listened to the hushed voices behind the door. Finally, Quinty emerged, wiping his hands on a white handkerchief. He smiled when he saw us.

"I'm Quinty. I recognize you, Sheriff Astrid. You and Britta look too much alike not to." He squinted at me. "You don't look familiar, I'm afraid. And you don't look enough like Astrid to be another sister."

"Is there somewhere we can talk privately?" Astrid asked.

"Let's go upstairs," he said. "That way I know we won't be interrupted." He turned to Pansy. "Please make sure no one disturbs us."

Pansy returned to her seat. "Of course."

Quinty gestured for us to follow him. We walked to a curved staircase that I realized was simply hanging in the air. There were no support beams visible anywhere. Markos would love to see a design like this.

"Pansy is your sister, isn't she?" Astrid asked.

Quinty glanced at her over his shoulder. "How did you know?"

"You have that subtle animosity that only seems to come

with siblings," Astrid replied. "Plus you yelled at her when she opened your office door. It seems like the kind of thing you do to a family member rather than a proper employee."

We reached the next floor where Quinty gave Astrid a full smile. "You're very good, Sheriff. Now tell me how I can help you. I assume Britta isn't with you for a reason."

Astrid nodded. "We need to ask you some questions. I figured it would be best if we weren't distracted by pre-existing relationships."

Quinty frowned. "Now I'm concerned. This sounds serious."

He walked further into the room and I gasped. The ceilings were easily fifteen feet high and the floor was one massive room full of inventions. I could have spent hours in here and not seen everything. I spotted a magical washboard that appeared to operate by itself. A tie that knotted itself. A full-sized box that folded up small enough to fit in your pocket when not in use.

"This place is amazing," I said. A blush crept into my cheeks. "Sorry, I didn't mean to get off topic. I've heard you're very talented and you worked wonders on my Volvo, but this place is something else."

Quinty folded his arms and beamed with pride. He was, like his sister, slight in stature and very elf-like. "Volvo, did you say?"

I nodded. "Daniel brought it to you. You guys fished it out of Swan Lake."

Quinty wagged a finger at me. "You're the famous Emma Hart." He jammed his hands into his trouser pockets. "Wow. I can't believe it. It is so nice to finally meet you. I've heard a lot of good things about you."

"Same here," I said.

Astrid cleared her throat. "When we're finished with the lovefest, I have some important news to share with Quinty."

I immediately felt guilty for hijacking the conversation. "Of course. Sorry, Astrid."

Astrid fixed her attention on Quinty. "I'm afraid I have some bad news. It seems that one of your employees was found dead yesterday morning."

Quinty's mouth dropped open. "I only have two employees out today and I spoke to one of them this morning." His expression clouded over. "That leaves Walter."

"I'm afraid so," Astrid confirmed. "We're working to identify the cause of death, but it looks like murder."

Quinty began to choke. "Murder? Are you sure?"

"Not yet," Astrid admitted. "But it looks likely."

Quinty covered his face with his hands. "I can't believe it. Poor Marianne." He yanked his hands away and stared at us. "Dear gods. Does she know?"

Astrid nodded. "She didn't seem to think Walter had an enemy in the world. We thought we would talk to you and see if you had the same impression."

Quinty paced the floor in front of us, dragging his fingers through his spiky hair. "I do. Walter was the most jovial troll you'd ever want to meet. It was one of the reasons we worked so well together. Usually elves and trolls are at loggerheads, but Walter was different."

That matched what his wife had said.

"Did he have any issues with other employees? Maybe an argument that carried over into their personal lives?" Astrid asked.

"Not that I can think of," he said. "You'd have to ask Pansy. She's much more aware of office politics than I am. I tend to have my head in the clouds most of the time."

"When I was in the human world, I went to Thomas Edison's workshop," I said. "This place is like a magical version of his."

Quinty gaped at me. "You've been to Thomas Edison's workshop?"

"When I was younger. My grandparents took me. My grandfather was an admirer of his."

"Who wasn't?" Quinty appeared momentarily stunned. "Gosh, I would love to talk to you more about that when you have time. Edison is one of my heroes. I've read all the books on him in the library."

"Really?" Looking around his magical workshop, I couldn't imagine what Quincy could learn from a human inventor. It showed how naïve I was about such things.

"Absolutely," Quinty replied. "What an opportunity. Let me know when you'd like to hang out and I will probably ask lots of questions you won't remember the answers to." He chuckled softly. "Man, poor Walter. This is a huge blow."

"We'll speak to Pansy on the way out, if that's okay," Astrid said.

Quinty nodded, already lost in inventive thought.

Astrid and I made our way back down the curved staircase to the reception desk. Pansy was filling out some paperwork with her quill and ink. She glanced up when she heard us approach.

"Everything okay?" she asked.

Astrid leaned on the desk. "Unfortunately not. We have some bad news. Walter Rivers was found dead yesterday morning. We were hoping you might be able to tell us if you're aware of any problems between Walter and anyone in the office."

Pansy's face paled and she seemed unable to move.

"I'm so sorry, Pansy," I said. "We hate to deliver news this way, but we're trying to figure out what happened to him. Any information you can give would be helpful."

Pansy remained immobile. Astrid and I exchanged glances, uncertain how to proceed.

"Pansy," I prodded. "Can I get you anything? A drink?"

She seemed to register my words. "No," she choked out. "What happened to him?"

"He was found in the forest near Larkspur Bridge," Astrid said. "He was frozen to death. We're trying to determine the nature of his condition, whether a spell was used. We don't have all the information yet, but we spoke to his wife and we want to speak to his workplace colleagues as well."

Pansy sucked in a breath. "Aside from Quinty, Walter was the most popular guy here. He never had a bad word to say about anyone." She squeezed her eyes closed. "Who would do this to him?"

"I take it you two were close," I said. Her reaction was more intense then a simple employee relationship. It stood to reason that they'd developed a tight bond over the years.

"Well, I've seen him almost every day for years on end," Pansy said quietly. "You get to know someone when you spend that much time with him."

"Why don't we give you a chance to collect your thoughts?" Astrid said. "When you're ready to talk, come down to my office. Or I'd be happy to come back here. Whatever works best for you."

Pansy inhaled sharply and nodded. She seemed to be struggling to breathe normally.

"Maybe go upstairs and talk to your brother when we leave," I suggested. "Don't just sit here and try to carry on like everything is normal." That wasn't a healthy response. Not that I was an expert in healthy communication.

Pansy gave a crisp nod. "I will. Thank you."

Astrid and I barely made it out the door when we heard her convulsive sobs behind us.

"There's more to that story," Astrid said quietly.

I agreed. If we bided our time, we'd find out what it was soon enough.

CHAPTER 9

As I passed through the town square on my way back to the office, a familiar set of broad shoulders grabbed my attention.

"Daniel," I called before I could stop myself.

He turned to me, flashing an angelic smile, and my heart skipped a beat. I wondered if there would ever come a day when I looked at him and felt nothing. It seemed impossible.

"You look energized," he said. "Have you been getting your fix in Brew-Ha-Ha?"

"Not today," I said. "Too busy for a leisurely latte."

"Me too." He held up a hanger with a garment bag. "Just picked up my wedding suit. Want to see it?"

The enthusiasm in his turquoise eyes told me that the Obsession potion was still in his system. What was taking so long?

"Oh, I wouldn't want anything to happen to it," I lied. "Best to keep it covered up when you're outside."

"Good point. Elsa would murder me if I ruined the suit before the wedding."

No, she'd likely murder me and dance on my corpse in her wedding shoes.

"Are you nervous about the big day?" I asked. I hated making small talk about my nightmare, but it seemed like the only thing to do right now.

He puffed out his chest. "I feel great. Elsa is an incredible fairy. I'm lucky to have her."

Inwardly I winced. *No, Elsa is lucky to have you.*

"I'm sure it will be a very grand affair," I said, trying to keep my tone neutral. "Elsa doesn't seem to do understated."

"No," he said with a short laugh. "She really doesn't. She's my fancy fairy."

The longer we spoke, the angrier I became. Something must have happened with the mayor. I couldn't understand why Daniel was still obsessed. It made no sense.

"Elsa is controlling the seating chart at the country club, but I made sure she didn't stick you at the dwarves' table."

"I like dwarves. What's wrong with that?"

He grinned. "You haven't attended a Spellbound wedding yet, have you?"

A lump formed in my throat and I struggled to speak. "No." And now my first one would be the worst one I could possibly imagine.

"Dwarves are notorious for drinking too much and causing chaos at weddings. You're not a bridesmaid, though, so you should be safe, though you may be pretty enough to be a target." He winked at me and my insides melted.

"Thanks for the tip," I said. "I'll be sure to steer clear."

I gazed at him a beat too long and he broke into a broad smile. "Everything okay? You seem dazed."

I seemed dazed? Ugh. The cruel irony.

"Sorry." I desperately tried to shake his hold on me. "Lost in thought. I, um, need to go see the mayor about a town council issue."

"You're heading in the wrong direction then," Daniel said.

"Yes, I realize that." There was no saving face. I just had to embrace the idiot I appeared to be. "I'll talk to you soon."

"Hope so," he said. "I miss our chats."

I felt a pang of longing in my chest. "Me too."

I spun on my heel and hurried to the Mayor's Mansion before he could see the tears glistening in my eyes. I didn't care if the mayor was in her underwear in the middle of a dress fitting. She was going to explain herself to me —right now.

Luckily for me, I didn't need to walk all the way to the mansion.

"Speak of the devil and she appears," I said, as the mayor came toward me, flanked by her two hounds, Zeus and Hera.

Her expression hardened when she saw me. "Nice to see you, dear. I hear you're quite busy these days with a nasty case of indecent exposure."

As I advanced toward her, Hera growled. I took a careful step backward. "I just ran into Daniel, who still seems very excited about his upcoming wedding. Even had his wedding suit. Care to explain?"

"Not really," she said dismissively. "I owe you nothing."

When she attempted to flutter past me, I blocked her path. "What's going on? Why haven't you done anything?"

"I did *something*," the mayor said. "Just not what you wanted."

My stomach dropped. "What do you mean? Where's the vial?"

"The vial has been taken care of," she replied coolly. "And Elsa has taken steps to insure that no one finds the others."

I gaped at the imperious fairy. "I don't understand. You don't want this wedding to happen any more than I do."

"No, I don't. But I've weighed that outcome against what

would happen to Elsa if anyone found out and I've landed on the side of sucking up to a new son-in-law."

I couldn't believe what I was hearing. "We had a deal. You…you can't do this."

"I can and I have," the mayor replied simply.

My body was rigid with fear and panic. The vial was gone. The mayor was no longer on my side and Elsa knew what I'd done. The lengths I was willing to go to. This turn of events did not bode well for me.

"I'll tell everyone the truth," I sputtered.

"What truth? You have no proof. It would be your word against the mayor's." She gave me a pointed look. "An extremely popular mayor who's been a selfless pillar of the community for many, many years. Is that truly a battle you think you can win, new witch? It doesn't matter how much residents like you. You're still an unknown entity, whereas I have a longstanding reputation here."

She was right. In a popularity contest, Mayor Knightsbridge would win hands down.

I gulped. "And I don't suppose I get my committee either."

"I may still give it to you as a consolation prize." She studied me for a moment. "You should consider yourself fortunate, dear, to have escaped Daniel's clutches. He's not worthy of you. He's not worthy of my Elsa either, but if she wants him, I won't stand in her way."

"No, you'll act as her accomplice," I snapped.

Mayor Knightsbridge's jaw tensed. "There's no need for hostility, dear. We're all friends here. When you live long enough, you'll learn that you can't always get what you want."

Live long enough? I'd learned that hard truth when I lost my mother at three years old. And I'd learned it all over again when I was seven. I didn't need some haughty fairy to teach me life lessons.

"Maybe if you had taught your daughter that valuable lesson early on, then we wouldn't be in this mess now."

The mayor's mouth twitched. "See you at the wedding, dear. I'll be sure to have extra tissues on hand for those so inclined to express regret."

She brushed past me, her hounds hot on her heels.

I continued to stand there, my hopes and dreams crashing down around me. The invisibility spell had been for nothing. The evidence was gone. The mayor was no longer an ally. I felt like dissolving into the cobblestone. I'd blown my chance to bring Elsa down.

An image of Daniel flashed in my mind. His engaging smile. The look of surprise in his eyes when he'd kissed me at the high school dance. There was a real connection between us. I couldn't give up on him.

Although Magpie would hate me for saying this, there was more than one way to skin a cat.

CHAPTER 10

I STRETCHED out on my bed and stared at the ceiling. Life seemed so hopeless. I hadn't felt this awful since my father died. I grabbed a pillow and stuffed it over my face to block out the world.

"I don't think that's the most effective way to kill yourself." Gareth's muffled voice penetrated the feather-stuffed barrier.

"I'm not trying to kill myself," I replied.

"What's that now? I can't understand a word."

I tossed the pillow aside. "I'm not trying to kill myself. I'm trying to block out the sounds of my abject failure."

"Then let's focus on something positive for a change," Gareth said, hovering beside the bed. "Firstly, I have helpful information for you."

I sat up quickly. "About Daniel?"

"No, sorry," he said. "About the murder case. Walter Rivers."

I squinted at him. "You have information about Walter?"

"Aye. I manifested in the library again and overheard

someone gossiping about Walter's neighbor. It seems that he and Walter were at odds over something. Not sure what."

"Which neighbor?" I asked.

"I only heard the name Jeremiah."

"Thanks, Gareth. That's actually incredibly helpful."

"Don't sound so surprised," he scoffed.

"What's secondly?"

"Eh?"

"You said 'firstly,' which implies there's a 'secondly.'"

His expression brightened. "Oh, yes. Secondly, I'd like to help you with the committee."

"What committee?" I asked glumly.

"The committee you've been fighting for. The one to revise the sentencing guidelines," he replied. "I'd be an invaluable resource for you."

I pulled my knees to my chest. "I have no doubt that you would, but I don't think the mayor plans to stick to her promise." Since she already broke the most important promise of all.

"Why don't you report her to the council?" Gareth urged. "What she's done is reprehensible."

"Who's going to believe me?" I asked. "The mayor has a solid reputation. She isn't like Sheriff Hugo."

"True," Gareth agreed. "But people like you too. They trust you."

"Do they?" I wasn't so certain. "I think they're starting to, but I'm still a newcomer. Most people are probably waiting to make up their minds."

"I made up my mind the day we met," Gareth said.

"You're a special case," I replied. "I'm the only one who can see you. You didn't have a choice."

"What about Markos?" Gareth asked. "He made up his mind by the end of the first date, I suspect."

"It wasn't a date," I insisted.

"What about when Daniel marries Elsa?" Gareth queried. "Will you give the minotaur with the tight buns a chance then?"

"Firstly, it's *if* the wedding takes place, not when."

"Semantics," Gareth said with a dismissive wave.

"Secondly…" I paused. "I can't invest in that type of negative thinking."

Gareth gestured to the pillow. "Methinks you already have."

Argh. I had to pull myself together. Shoving a pillow over my face was not going to solve my problems. I had to be stronger than this.

"Daniel is *not* going to marry Elsa," I said. "I won't allow it."

Gareth arched an eyebrow. "Won't allow it, eh? Fighting words from the upstart witch."

They were fighting words, and I meant every one. I had to find a way to stop Elsa from ruining Daniel's life. With her, he could never be the angel he wanted to be. He'd never get his halo back. Elsa was too selfish to help him achieve his dream of redemption. She only wanted to control him. To own him like a pet. It sickened me. Maybe if I tapped into my sorceress powers…but I couldn't. Not without revealing my true nature. Daniel deemed the risk too great. On the other hand, if the risk meant I could save him, then maybe it was worth it?

"Gareth…" I wanted so desperately to tell him. If anyone refused to judge me, it would be Gareth. As a gay dead undead Scottish vampire, he understood stereotypes and the downside of ignorance all too well.

"What is it?"

Daniel's warning echoed in my head. That I would be feared and misunderstood. That I would be shunned. If the worst happened, I had nowhere to go. I was trapped in Spell-bound just like everyone else.

"Nothing," I mumbled. "Just feeling insecure is all."

"From powerful to insecure in twenty seconds flat," Gareth mused. "I suppose it's a skill somewhere."

I shrugged. "What can I say? I'm a complicated human being."

"You forgot annoying," Gareth said.

"Hey!" I elbowed him playfully and was pleased to bump against something vaguely solid. "Check that out."

"I know," he said proudly. "It takes a fair bit of concentration, but I can add dimension when I put forth the effort."

"Did Lyra say it's possible for you to be permanently corporeal again?" I asked.

"It won't work like that," he replied. "I'll always be a ghost, but I'll be able to interact more on this plane than I've been able to so far."

This plane. "Is there anywhere else you can go? I mean, I know they wouldn't admit you to the afterlife, but are there other planes of existence you can visit aside from this one?"

"Even my ghost is trapped in Spellbound, you know that."

"I know, but the curse can't extend beyond this plane of existence, can it?" If it could, then that was one almighty curse.

"I suppose not," he admitted. "But I'm not aware of any other planes to visit. When I practice leaving the house, I focus on my next destination. I sort of blink and find myself there."

"Well, it's nice to see you gaining weight," I joked.

Gareth pretended to suck in his stomach. "Aye. It truly is. And that's the only time you'll ever hear that from me."

"If this committee ever gets off the ground," I said, "how about I hold the meetings here, until you can appear in more places?"

"But no one will be able to see me or hear me except you," Gareth complained. "And you'll be too busy running the meetings to translate."

I tapped my chin. "Then I'll invite Kassandra to attend as well. She can act as your translator." Kassandra was a psychic that could channel Gareth. Although her abilities weren't as straightforward as mine, they were better than nothing.

Gareth's expression softened. "Really? You'd do that for me?"

"Of course I would. You're my vampire ghost roommate."

He broke into a smile, showing his fangs. "Or perhaps simply 'my roommate' would suffice."

"You're my roommate and I wouldn't have it any other way," I said, and gave him the best hug possible. At least my arms didn't completely slide through him.

Magpie appeared out of nowhere and thrust himself between us like a child in need of attention.

"I think someone else would prefer to have it another way," Gareth remarked wryly.

"Sorry, Magpie," I said. "But I have it on good authority that we can't always get what we want."

Magpie looked up at me and hissed.

With the wedding creeping up on the calendar, I developed a renewed sense of urgency. Even without the vial, I was determined to try and create an Anti-Obsession potion that cured Daniel.

"How can we mix an Anti-Obsession potion if we don't know exactly which Obsession potion Elsa is using?" Laurel asked.

"Mom said we have to experiment," Sophie said. "Keep trying different permutations until we find the right mixture that counteracts Elsa's."

"But how will we get Daniel to keep drinking potions?" Millie asked. "He's going to be suspicious if we're pouring strange liquids down his gullet."

I sighed. "And Elsa will be watching him like a hawk now that she realizes I know the truth."

Begonia's eyes brightened. "There'll be a bachelor party, right? What if we prepared all the possible combinations in advance and made sure to slip each one into one of his drinks during the party?"

"That's a great idea," I said.

"Except we wouldn't be invited to his bachelor party," Millie said, ever the sourpuss.

"Who needs an invitation?" I queried. "Desperate times call for desperate measures."

"We need to find out when and where it will be held," Laurel said.

"Plus we've got to get all the possible potions ready," Sophie added. "That will take time."

"And research," Laurel said, her eyes shining with excitement. Maybe the rest of us didn't know what our specialties would be, but I was pretty sure I could guess Laurel's.

"I still can't believe the mayor stabbed you in the back like that," Begonia said. "If the truth ever comes out, she's going to be on Swan Lake without a paddle."

"She said if it's her word against mine that she'll win," I said, flopping onto the sofa. "And I'm sure she's right. We can't rely on her. We need to find another way to stop the wedding."

"Talk about unconditional love," Millie grumbled. "The mayor has a pristine reputation. Now she's going to destroy it because she raised a selfish brat."

"I don't understand her long-term plan," Laurel said. "Is she going to allow Elsa to stay married to Daniel under false pretenses for the rest of their lives?"

"Apparently," I said. "She thinks having Daniel for a son-in-law is preferable to having a disgraced daughter."

Begonia made a face. "I'm so disappointed in the mayor. I really looked up to her until this."

I groaned. "The whole thing is awful. Let's find out the details on the bachelor party. Who's the best person to ask?" The best person wasn't Daniel. I didn't want him to tip off Elsa.

"We should go to the Horned Owl and ask around," Sophie said. "The bartenders know all the gossip."

"And you can flirt with the bartender," Begonia said, lightly punching Sophie's arm.

"One of the perks of helping a friend," Sophie said with a smile.

"We should go now before the post-work crowd swarms the place," Millie said.

"And you can get a stool right at the bar," Begonia said to Sophie. "An unobstructed view of your favorite satyr."

Sophie turned scarlet. "Please don't tease me in front of him. I'll be mortified."

"I should probably head home," Laurel said. "I won't be allowed to drink anyway." She gathered her belongings together. "I can focus on Anti-Obsession potions tonight if you don't mind me working on them alone."

I was touched. "Laurel, you're thirteen years old. You should be doing something fun. Go home and play a game with your siblings."

"My siblings are irritating," Laurel said. "Besides, I want to help. I feel like I'm the weak link in the remedial witch chain."

"Laurel, that's ridiculous," I said. "You're so smart, not to mention a crucial member of the team."

She hugged her backpack to her chest. "Even so, I'd feel better if I made a solid contribution to the cause for once."

Begonia clapped her on the shoulder. "Have at it, Laurel. Let us know how you make out."

Laurel glanced at Sophie. "And be sure to let me know *if* you make out."

Sophie covered her ears. "I am not hearing this from a thirteen-year-old. Your mother would turn me into a toad if I led you astray."

"I'm in the mood to be led astray," Begonia said brightly. "Let's go now before the feeling wears off."

We left the secret lair and headed to the Horned Owl... purely for investigative purposes, of course.

CHAPTER 11

THE NEXT MORNING I drove Sigmund over to the Rivers'
neighborhood and knocked on the door of the small cottage
with the rounded thatched roof. I bit back a smile as I
observed the arched front door. The whole thing reminded
me of the Smurfs' mushroom-shaped houses.

The front door squeaked open and a face peered out at
me from the darkness of the interior. "Yes?"

"Hi there. My name is Emma Hart and I'm here to ask a
couple of questions about your neighbor, Walter."

"Walter? You mean that thief of a neighbor of mine?"

"I take it you haven't heard the news then," I said.

The voice in the darkness hesitated. "What news?"

"Walter is dead, I'm afraid."

The door opened further until the figure was bathed in
sunlight. His beady eyes focused on me.

"Dead, did you say?"

"Yes, he was found by Larkspur Bridge. I'm surprised you
haven't heard."

"I tend to keep to myself," he replied. He seemed momentarily stunned. "Come on in. What did you say your name was again?"

I stepped over the threshold. The interior of the cottage was warm and comfortable, awash in earthy tones.

"Emma Hart," I repeated. "I'm helping Sheriff Astrid with the case."

"I'm Jeremiah Brown," he said.

I could tell he was a shifter, but I couldn't pinpoint which type.

"When was the last time you saw Walter?" I asked.

"Earlier this week," Jeremiah replied. "I went over to his house to get something that belonged to me."

"I see. And did he give it to you?"

Jeremiah's lips formed a thin line. "No. He said he couldn't yet."

"Do you mind if I ask what it was?"

"I suppose we should make ourselves comfortable." Jeremiah ambled over to a nearby chair and sat. He gestured for me to do the same.

"Do you always keep your house so dark?" I asked. Not even the vampires in town chose to live in a constant state of darkness.

"I'm a weremole," he explained. "Short of living underground, this is the next best thing."

"Why don't you live underground?" I asked. "There's no rule about that, is there?" Not that I would put it past the town to have such a rule in place.

Jeremiah chuckled. "I suppose I could now. I'm used to living here, though. It was my wife who needed to live above the ground. She was a pixie. She would've suffocated underground."

Even if he hadn't used the past tense to talk about her, I could tell by the expression on his face that his wife was deceased.

"I'm sorry, Jeremiah. I didn't realize."

He waved me off. "It's been four years now," he said. "I'm sure I could move out of the cottage, but it's where we spent our married life together. I couldn't bear to leave it. Too many good memories." He sniffed the air. "Her scent even lingers, you know?"

"I understand completely," I said. I remembered very distinctly not wanting to leave my house after my father died. There was no choice, though. My grandparents weren't going to move into the house when they already had a house of their own. So I moved.

"May I ask what happened?"

Jeremiah drew a deep breath. "It was an accident. Not sure if you know this, but pixie wings move real fast. Much faster than fairy wings. She was flying with a slower friend and turned around to say something and flew smack into the side of a building." He shook his head. "A pointless way to die."

"That's awful," I said. "I'm so sorry, Jeremiah."

He wiped a straight tear from his cheek. "I apologize. I still find it difficult to talk about."

"Don't apologize to me," I said. "Of course it's difficult. She was your wife and you loved her."

He sniffed and nodded. "That's why I was so angry with Walter. He knew how important those items were to me. I just wanted them back."

"Which items did he borrow?" I asked.

"Her wings."

I nearly choked on my saliva. "I'm sorry. Did you say her wings?"

"Yes. And also a jar of her pixie dust. I'd scraped together as much as I could find. She used to leave it lying around the house, you see. She wasn't exactly known for her neatness." He smiled to himself.

I tried to digest the information. "Why did you lend these items to Walter?"

"Because I knew he was working on an invention and thought they would be helpful. My wife would have liked the idea of contributing to something like that."

Paranormal organ donation.

I gave him a sympathetic smile. "And let me guess. You eventually had a change of heart."

Jeremiah nodded emphatically. "I couldn't sleep, knowing I didn't have her wings or her pixie dust. It started to feel wrong. I spoke to Walter about it and he agreed to return them."

"But then he refused?" I asked.

"He didn't so much refuse as dodge the request," Jeremiah replied. "He started avoiding me. I spoke to Marianne about it when he wasn't home, but she had no idea where he kept the items. We even looked in the house together."

"So when you confronted Walter at his house a few days ago, what happened?"

Jeremiah scratched his head. "He promised to get them for me, but he said he needed some time."

"And were you willing to give him that?"

"I was angry. I'll admit that much. You have to understand —we're talking about a piece of my wife. It felt like I handed over one of my own limbs and he wouldn't give it back. I know I offered them in the first place so I wasn't being fair… " He trailed off. "We don't always act rationally when emotions are involved."

No, we certainly didn't.

"It's okay, Jeremiah," I said. "I'm not here to judge you. I think anyone in your position would feel the same. It was generous of you to offer them in the first place."

"I didn't even know what he was working on, but I trusted him," Jeremiah said. "Pretty stupid, right?"

"No, not stupid at all. I have a feeling that your wife would have approved."

Jeremiah pressed his lips together, clearly thinking of her. "She would have. She loved talking to Walter about his inventions. If you don't mind my asking, how did he die?"

"He froze to death," I said. "Sheriff Astrid suspects foul play. The lab report shows traces of magic."

"Is that so? Then I guess you're looking for a magic user," Jeremiah said. "And I am definitely not that."

"Neither was Walter, but that didn't stop him from working with pixie dust."

Jeremiah blinked his beady eyes. "You think I'm a suspect?"

"Not anymore," I said.

Jeremiah seemed surprised. "I could be lying to you. Why do you believe me?"

"We all have our skills," I said. "I happen to be a decent judge of character."

Jeremiah nodded approvingly. "Do me a favor," he said. "If you happen to find my wife's wings and the jar of pixie dust, will you return them to me?"

"As long as the sheriff approves it, then yes. Definitely."

He closed his eyes gently, relieved. "Thank you."

CHAPTER 12

I ENTERED the Grapevine Room of the Spellbound Country Club. I learned from the bartender in the Horned Owl that it was the upscale bar and restaurant in the club. Since Daniel wasn't even a member here, I had no doubt that Elsa had made the arrangements. Of course she chose a very masculine environment—the room screamed metrosexual steakhouse. No succubi strippers in g-strings and cheap feather boas for Daniel.

I hated to come alone, but I knew that a group of remedial witches would draw too much attention at a bachelor party and I didn't want my friends implicated if anything went awry. It would have been different if the party had taken place at the Horned Owl because we're regulars there. I'd never been to the Grapevine Room before. Even now, I'd concocted a plausible story for showing up here.

"Emma? What on heaven and earth are you doing here?"

Stars and stones, Daniel looked incredibly handsome in a hot pink polo shirt and neatly pressed trousers. His rugged jawline was covered in attractive scruff.

"I'm waiting for Gareth," I lied. "He's been making an

effort to materialize here. The Grapevine Room was one of his favorite places."

"Oh." He looked around as though seeing it for the first time. "It is nice in here, isn't it?"

"And busy." I nodded toward the crowd surrounding the bar.

He shrugged. "Apparently you discover you have more friends than you realize when it's your bachelor party."

"At least they're here to have fun." I recognized a slew of faces. Demetrius Hunt and his vampire circle. Former sheriff and resident grumpy centaur, Hugo.

"You look pretty tonight," he said, admiring my simple black shift dress. "Black suits you."

"Thank you," I replied, resisting the urge to melt into a puddle. "What's with the halfhearted attempt at a beard?"

He rubbed his jaw. "You like it?"

"I do, actually." Crap on a stick. I really did. Could he try to be less appealing and make my life easier?

"It won't last long," he said. "Elsa hates it. I only have it so I can have a nice, clean shave on our wedding day."

At the mention of their wedding day, my whole body stiffened and I remembered why I was here. I felt the weight of the vials pressed against my thigh.

"What are you drinking?" I asked. "I'll buy us a round."

"That's kind of you," he said. "I don't want you to go to any trouble."

"No trouble at all," I said. "How about you start slow and steady with an ale?"

"Perfect. Thanks."

I hurried to the bar and ordered an ale for Daniel and a bucksberry fizz for me.

"You're celebrating this debacle?" Demetrius sidled up next to me, oozing his usual sex appeal.

"Of course not. I'm just trying to be a supportive friend."

He eyed me carefully. "You're up to something."

The bartender set my order in front of me. "Please start a tab," I said. "I'm planning to stay awhile."

Demetrius glanced at the drinks and back to me. "Okay. You're *definitely* up to something."

I gave an innocent shrug of my shoulders. "Demetrius Hunt, whatever do you mean?" Quickly I glanced around. "Now be a good vampire and look away for a second."

He chuckled and did as instructed. I slid the first vial from my pocket and tipped the contents into the ale. I sniffed the beverage to make sure there was no strange odor. I smelled only the ale.

"Okay, it's safe to look."

He turned back to me. "I don't know what you're up to, but please let it involve a stripper pole and magical boobs."

"Sorry, Dem. Not tonight." I patted his arm. "Wish me luck." I returned to Daniel and handed over the pint glass. "Bottoms up."

"Yours looks good, too," he said. "It's nice to see you enjoying yourself. I feel like you've been off lately."

That was an understatement. "If you're happy, then I'm happy. I only want the best for you, Daniel. You know that, right?"

He leaned down and kissed me on the cheek. "I know it's meant to be a bachelor party, but it wouldn't be the same without you."

As he drank the rest of the ale, I watched for any signs of change. Briefly I wondered whether Elsa had upped his dosage today, realizing that she wouldn't be with him tonight. She was exactly the kind of paranoid person who would go to such extreme measures. According to Sophie's mother, Elsa didn't actually need to keep pumping the potion into his system for it to be effective. Her method was overkill. Then again, overkill was Elsa's middle name.

"Have you seen Elsa's wedding dress?" I asked. I figured I'd ask a question about her and see how he reacted.

"Definitely not. She'd murder me." He laughed. "I'm sure she'll look beautiful no matter what she wears."

I tasted a tiny bit of vomit in my mouth. Ugh, wrong potion. I'd have to try again. If I didn't play my cards right, this could take a few excruciating hours. I didn't have hours.

"This feels far too civilized," I said. "In the human world, bachelor parties are crazy."

"Crazy how?" Daniel asked.

"Let's line up some shots," I said. "You wait here and I'll get them set up for you at the bar." And add a vial to each one. It was the quickest and most effective way to sort this out.

His brow furrowed. "I don't know. Shots?"

I squeezed his arm. "Yes, shots. It's a rite of passage for bachelors. You have to do it."

He grinned. "If you insist."

I edged my way back to the bar and ordered a row of shots.

"All the same?" the bartender queried.

"No, go ahead and vary it. They're all for the groom."

The bartender set down six shot glasses and announced each liquid as he poured it. Devil May Care. Tongue Sucker. Horny Toad. Shifter Spice. Twisted Tail. And, appropriately, Angel Wings.

There was no way I could sneak the potions into all six shot glasses without someone noticing. This would take a touch of magic to disguise my sleight of hand. I pulled out my wand and subtly placed it in front of me on the bar top, pointed at the glasses.

"Double, double, toil and trouble/place me in a secret bubble." I felt the shift around me as the room fell silent and I knew that the spell had taken hold. No one would notice me or what I was doing. I retrieved the remaining vials from my pockets and tipped the contents of each one into a shot glass. Each time I emptied a vial, I said a silent prayer that this would be the one to work. Once I'd finished, I tossed the vials over the bar into the open trashcan and reversed the bubble spell.

"Daniel," I called over my shoulder. "Shots are ready." And I was more than ready to end Elsa's influence over him.

He joined me at the bar and his turquoise eyes widened at the sight of the six shot glasses.

"I don't feel up to this," he said. "Elsa will be upset if I throw up on her white carpet." He fixed his gaze on me. "I don't like to upset her."

I wanted to smack his cheek hard and snap him out of it. If only it was that simple.

"Daniel, you're celebrating your lifetime commitment to her," I said calmly. "She'll understand. After all, she's the one who set up this whole party, isn't she?"

He nodded slowly. "She's having a bachelorette party too. Not tonight though."

"And I bet she'll be doing shots until the sun comes up." I handed him the closest glass. "Let's see how fast you can down these, Halo Boy."

His mouth quirked. "I have a better idea." He waved over a few guys from the other end of the bar. "Shots are on me for the next ten minutes. Everybody drink up."

A cheer went up as the bartender scrambled to fill orders. The shots in front of us were quickly grabbed by unseen hands, except the one Daniel still held. I sighed inwardly. Please let that be the right one.

"Which kind is this?" he asked, sniffing the amber liquid.

"Angel Wings," I replied.

"Well, that's appropriate," he said good-naturedly.

I hoped so.

I watched anxiously as he tipped back the glass and polished off the alcohol.

"Nice?" I asked.

"My head's a little fuzzy," he said.

Fuzzy seemed like a good sign. "You know, we never talk about Elsa. What would you say is her best quality?"

Daniel appeared thoughtful. Was he wondering why I would ask such a ridiculous question? Was he trying to remember any of her good qualities because he couldn't think of a single one? My pulse quickened at the possibility.

"Her wonderful personality," he finally replied.

Blargh. Not the right potion.

I stared at the empty bar top in front of us where the other shot glasses had been. Another opportunity lost. I slumped forward, contemplating the end of all my hopes and dreams. And I couldn't even move away. I was stuck in this town for eternity, forced to witness Daniel live an unfulfilled life. It was too painful to envision.

"What do you mean you don't want another drink?" I heard a voice ask. "It's your favorite hobby."

I turned to locate the source of the conversation. A middle-aged elf was talking to a dwarf, presumably her husband judging by the way they interacted.

"I don't know," the dwarf said. "I had a shot of something bitter but now I don't want anything else to drink. Ever."

Uh oh. It seemed that the dwarf's obsession with alcohol was being curbed by the potion. A good thing, perhaps?

"Let's go home," the dwarf said. "I don't feel like staying out late."

The elf looked delighted by her husband's remark. "Not even an ale for the road?"

He made a gagging noise and she clapped her hands gleefully as they left the room.

I began to eavesdrop on other conversations to see

79

whether anyone else was affected. Between Daniel and the dwarf, there were four more shots unaccounted for. It was ironic that if Daniel's obsession had been a natural one, then any of the Anti-Obsession potions would have done the trick. It was only because I was combatting a specific magic potion that it had to be the right combination of ingredients. Pfft. Magic.

"Hey, you went a whole sentence without mentioning Fiona," a satyr said to his dryad friend. "I think it's a new record."

I moved closer to their high top table to listen.

The dryad shrugged and drank his pint of ale. "I can go a whole sentence. In fact, I bet I can go the rest of the night."

"Really?" the satyr didn't seem convinced. "She's all you've talked about for weeks. You haven't shut up about her all night until now."

"I guess it just occurred to me that she's not that special."

The satyr wore a baffled expression. "Dude, if I didn't know you better, I'd think you were playing mind games with me." The satyr shook his head and finished his drink. "At least Fiona will be happy. She was getting tired of you sending her messages. Apparently, your owl kept pooping on her porch and she'd need to clean it up after a long day of cleaning her clients' houses."

"Then she'll be pleased to learn there will be no more messages," the dryad replied.

Okay, three more to go. I threaded my way through the crowd, listening intently.

"What do you mean you don't like that shirt? You insist on wearing it every time we go out. I'm surprised it hasn't sprouted legs and walked away."

Two left.

"I'll bet you fifty gold coins you can't resist biting your nails in the next ten minutes," a centaur said.

"Bring it on," his werewolf companion said. "The only thing I want to gnaw on right now is a juicy piece of steak. We should sit down and order."

And one more.

It took a few minutes, but I found the final recipient of the potion standing in front of the magical music player.

"Why are you trying to stop your song from playing?" the vampire asked. "You play it on repeat every time we're here. It annoys everyone."

"Then why are you so concerned?" the other vampire shot back. "Just be grateful I don't want to hear the song anymore. Ever again."

"Believe me, I am."

I felt a strong hand on my shoulder and whipped around.

"I've been looking for you," Daniel said. "You wandered off after the shots."

"Sorry, I wanted to mingle." Did I just use the word mingle? It made me sound like a refugee from the 1970s. "Are you having fun?"

He cocked his head. "I guess so. This isn't really me, though, you know?"

Boy did I ever. "Why don't you go home?"

"Because Elsa will know I left early and I'll feel like I let her down."

"Can't you go to your own house?"

He stroked his stubbled chin. "I hadn't really thought of that. I guess I can, although Elsa prefers that I stay with her."

No doubt.

"She misses me when I'm not around," he said with an apologetic grin. "I don't want to upset her. I'll hang out here for a little longer and then go to her house."

My spirits sank. There was nothing more I could do here tonight.

Demetrius appeared beside us holding two full glasses. "You both look like you could use a drink."

What was that saying—if you can't beat 'em, join 'em? I accepted the beverage and took a defeated gulp.

"Come back to the bar," Demetrius said. "A group of us are taking bets on which vampire has the longest fangs. We're about to do the measurements."

That sounded oddly entertaining. I glanced at Daniel. "Are you game?"

He clinked his glass against mine. "Why not?"

I gulped down the rest of the alcohol and my mind went cloudy. "And I'll have another drink while we're at it." At this point, the cloudier, the better.

CHAPTER 13

I sat in my office with my forehead resting on the desk. My meeting with Buck had just finished and I was taking a moment to clear the cobwebs from my head and the cotton from my mouth. Magical hangovers were so much worse than human ones.

"Do I need to send for a hangover potion?" Althea asked, poking her head in the doorway. "You look like Death ran over you and then backed up and did it again, just to be sure."

I knew her assessment was accurate because Buck didn't even attempt to hit on me during our meeting. When a werewolf with as much testosterone as Buck keeps his distance, you know you're not looking your best.

"I'll be fine," I said unconvincingly. I should have taken something before I left the house this morning. I hadn't been thinking clearly. My mind was fuzzy with the bachelor party and my failure to find the right Anti-Obsession potion. "I'm going to add a few notes to the file and go home."

A knock on the door suggested otherwise.

"Who is it?" Althea called.

The door opened and Alex stepped into my office. He took one look at me and balked.

"Is this a bad time?" he asked.

I waved him forward. "Do not fear the woman behind the mess."

Hesitantly, Alex took a seat across from me. His jeans were so tight that I was surprised he could sit without being uncomfortable. Not that I minded the view. Even vampires without a pulse wouldn't mind that view.

"Buck left a few minutes ago. We're working on his defense."

"I know. That's the reason I'm here."

Oh. "Do you have information that would help us?"

"I wish I did. I need this to get resolved in Buck's favor. The shifter community is getting worked up over it."

That was news to me. "Because of an indecent exposure charge? It's not that serious."

Alex heaved a sigh. "It's just one more blemish on the werewolf record. The pack doesn't like it."

"What about Lorenzo Mancini? Why is he not here to see me?" As the official leader of the werewolf pack, I wasn't sure why Alex was acting as pack spokeswolf.

"It's because of his position on the town council," Alex explained. "The pack thought it best if I represented everyone's concerns."

That made sense. Lorenzo's hands were tied. He didn't have the power to change any laws, not by himself. Nor did he want the appearance of impropriety.

"How can I help?" I asked. "Outside of defending Buck, I'm not sure what else I can do."

He tapped his foot anxiously on the floor. "I heard you're spearheading a committee, something about revising the harsh sentences. Maybe you could throw this ordinance into the mix and see how people react."

I tapped my quill on the desk. "The committee won't be changing any laws or ordinances. It's about revising the punishment for the ones that are already on the books."

Alex appeared disappointed. "Oh. Well, is there anything you can do about these ordinances? They target shifters and it isn't right."

I laughed. "You seem to think I have far more power than I do. I'm a public defender. I don't make the laws or the ordinances here. I just defend those accused of violating them."

Alex rubbed his hands on the arms of the chair. "I don't like seeing the pack bent out of shape. These ordinances make them feel persecuted. There's no rule that prevents witches from flying on broomsticks."

"To be fair, witches on broomsticks aren't leaving a trail of urine across someone's yard."

"No," Alex said, "but once in a while they might leave a trail of vomit." He gave me a pointed look.

Heat rushed to my cheeks. "Once in a blue moon that might happen." Or every time I flew. Whichever. "And I am only one person."

Alex smiled. "I'm not trying to give you a hard time. Honest. You know I like you, Emma. But I don't like the way things are shaking out around here. Makes the pack uncomfortable."

"Have you spoken to Lorenzo about it? He must have an opinion."

Alex pressed his lips together, as though unsure whether to continue. Finally he spoke. "I think Lorenzo is worried about losing his seat on the council. He doesn't want to speak up too much for the pack if it ruffles too many wings."

It never occurred to me that having the heads of the coven, the werewolf pack, and the vampire coven on the town council might be problematic. In a situation like this, it seemed impossible for Lorenzo to best represent his pack if he was concerned with losing his seat on the council.

"I think you should petition the town council to change the ordinances," I suggested. "You're unhappy about the shifting restrictions too, right? Draft a list of which ones you object to and how you would change them." In my experience, if you were going to complain about something, it was best to offer an alternative or a solution. Those complaints always seemed to be the most effective.

"And then what?" he asked. "Get on the agenda for the next town council meeting?"

I nodded. "Speak to Lucy, the mayor's assistant. Tell her I sent you. She's a good friend." *Just don't use my name within earshot of the mayor.*

Alex nodded. "I know who Lucy is. Hard not to notice a pretty fairy like that."

My romance radar pinged. "Lucy is adorable. She's single, you know."

Alex looked bashful. "Thanks for the tip, but you know I can't date outside my kind. Not if I expect to take over the pack one day."

"You'd sacrifice your personal happiness to run the pack?" I asked.

"That's the whole point of being part of a pack," he said. "You do what's best for the whole. We're only as strong as our weakest link."

"Yes, but if your strongest link is unhappy, doesn't that weaken the whole chain anyway?"

He wagged a finger at me. "Don't you go using your lawyer mind tricks on me, young lady." He chuckled. "Thanks for the help, Emma. I appreciate it. I know you'll do a good job defending Buck."

"I always do my best."

"That's all we can ask of anyone," Alex said, standing to

give me one more decent view of his tight jeans before he left my office.

By the time I reached Dr. Hall's office for my afternoon appointment, I was ready to crawl across the floor and curl up in the chaise lounge.

"If you take a nap, I'm still charging you for the session," Catherine said. She poured two Arrogant Bitches and handed one to me.

"It's disturbing how comfortable I'm getting with this arrangement," I said, taking a sip.

"Stick with me, Hart, and see the world from a whole different viewpoint." She plopped on the chair beside me and kicked off her shoes, making herself comfortable. I noticed her toenails were painted black with white skulls and crossbones.

"Pretty sure that happened when I arrived in Spellbound," I said.

She laughed and I realized how pretty she was when she didn't look sullen. "Good point." She swallowed a mouthful and peered at me with interest. "So how are you feeling about the disaster that is your life?"

I scowled. "That's a bit harsh."

She shrugged. "Is it? Seems pretty accurate to me. You're even starting to look like a walking disaster. I can't believe Gareth let you leave the house looking this way. Shame on him."

I brushed the stray hairs from the edge of my face in an effort to appear more presentable. "He wasn't around."

Catherine drained her glass and set it aside. "So how are you feeling about next Saturday?"

"What's next Saturday?" I asked, avoiding her steely gaze.

Without warning, her fangs popped out and she lunged

for me. I screamed and fell off the chaise lounge, landing hard on my bottom.

"What was that for?" I asked. Sulking, I rubbed my sore tailbone.

"Dishonesty" Catherine said, retracting her fangs and settling back in the chair. "Do it again and I *will* bite."

"Your methods are highly questionable," I said.

"And yet you keep turning up for appointments," she said. "I must be doing something right."

I returned to the chaise lounge and took another drink. "How do you think I feel? Awful. Sick. Terrified."

Catherine pointed at me. "Bingo."

"Bingo?"

"Terrified. Let's talk about that."

I cringed. "Do we have to?"

"Why are you terrified?"

"I think it's obvious," I said.

"Not to me. Pretend I don't have a PhD from one of the best vampire universities in the world."

I pinched the fabric of the cushion, forcing out the words. "Because Daniel is going to marry Elsa while he's under this stupid spell and there's nothing I can do to stop it. It's completely out of my control. I thought once I had the vial of Obsession potion, that would be enough to stop the madness."

"But you don't have the potion anymore?"

I shook my head. "Mayor Knightsbridge destroyed it."

Catherine narrowed her eyes. "Destroyed it? She's planning to let her daughter continue this charade?"

"Apparently."

"I never liked that uppity fairy. Too big for her wings." She stood and stretched her arms over her head. "Tell me more about your fear."

"What fear?" I asked. "There's nothing to fear but fear

itself."

"Who fed you that minotaur shit?" she shot back. "There are loads of things to be afraid of." She ticked them off on her fingers. "Snakes, being buried alive, a huge, unexpected tax bill, an enchantress with a grudge. The list goes on. What are you, Emma Hart, afraid of?"

I shuddered. "I used to have nightmares about being buried alive when I was a child."

"I *was* buried alive," Catherine said. "It's no picnic, I'll tell you that much. Luckily, I woke up as a vampire so I simply clawed my way out of the coffin. Easy peasy."

The thought was horrifying. "You were buried alive?"

Catherine returned to the bar to refresh her glass. "I guess technically I was dead and then I became undead."

"You still haven't told me the story of how you became a vampire."

She gave me a dismissive wave. "We're here to talk about you, honey."

"Are you sure about that?"

She ignored the question. "Fear. Go."

"I'm afraid of losing Daniel forever."

"The way you lost your parents forever?"

I nodded and sipped my drink. The alcohol warmed my stomach and I felt a little better. "Getting to know him filled a hole in me that I didn't even realize existed. To have to imagine a future without him…" I blinked back tears. "It's a dark place. I'd rather time stand still."

"You made it this far without your parents," Catherine said. "How did the future look after your father died?"

"I was seven," I replied. "I didn't have a concept of the future then. It was more about coming to terms with never seeing my father again."

"Daniel Starr isn't like your parents. He's immortal. An angel, remember? You'll be able to see him as long as you live. Of course, you'll see him married to someone else."

I buried my face in my hands. "Gee, thanks for the upbeat reminder."

Catherine shrugged. "If you love Daniel so much, you should just be grateful that he's here on earth, even if he's walking blindly among the living."

"But he deserves better than that."

"Why does it bother you so much?" she prodded. "If he's oblivious and seemingly content…"

"Because he doesn't belong with Elsa. It isn't right."

"Says who?"

My jaw tensed. "Do you mean to tell me that if Lord Gilder suddenly became engaged to someone like Lady Weatherby, you wouldn't be crying foul and screaming to the hilltops that it isn't right?"

"J.R. Weatherby?" Catherine scoffed. "Unlikely. She's not his type."

"Because you are?"

Catherine glared at me. "Stop trying to turn the tables. We're talking about your fear, not mine. If I were going to talk about fear, I'd talk about the time I was chained to a wall and left to starve. I didn't know when or if anyone would come to help me."

A lump formed in my throat at the thought of Catherine in such a dire situation. "Did that really happen?" It was hard to know with her.

"I remember every excruciating moment."

"You obviously escaped."

"Thank the devil. I was a vampire who got involved with the wrong guy."

"A human did that to you?" I asked, shocked.

"No, a self-loathing vampire. He tried to torture the vampirism out of me." She gave me a sad smile. "He'd been a preacher before he was turned and he had a difficult time with his…situation."

"And yours, apparently." Every time I thought my life was in the toilet, Catherine found a way to make it seem like a Sunday picnic compared with hers.

"So back to Daniel," she said. "What's the worst that can happen if he marries her and believes he loves her? If that's his reality, then is it so horrible?"

"Yes!" I struggled to find the right words. "He won't be living an authentic life if the love isn't real. The marriage will be a lie. A sham."

"But if he *believes* it to be real, is there actually a difference?"

I leaped to my feet. "Of course there's a difference. Daniel wants his halo restored. He wants to make amends and do good deeds to make up for past wrongs. He wants to be the best version of himself. He can't possibly do that if he's living a lie."

Catherine blew out a breath. "And let me guess, Miss Leaping Llama Drama—without him, you don't think you can be the best version of yourself either. His failure becomes your failure."

Was that what I believed? Maybe it was.

"I never in my wildest dreams believed I would ever meet anyone like him," I admitted.

"Because you lived in the human world?"

"No, because of our connection. It was immediate. I feel…" How could I describe the intense and yet soothing nature of our relationship? "I feel like we've always been a part of each other's lives. Being with him feels as natural as breathing."

Catherine scraped her knuckle along her cheek. "And now Elsa has cut off your oxygen supply?"

"Dr. Hall, are you…crying?"

She hissed and bared her fangs. "Of course not. Don't be absurd. Crying is for people about to be eaten." She shot me a guilty look. "I mean, sad people. Very sad."

"It's okay to be sad," I told her. "Sadness can be a healthy emotion, as long as it doesn't take over your life."

"Listen to you," she said, draining her second glass dry. "Only one of us has the degree in psychology, remember? No chaise lounge analysis, please."

"I think you should ask Lord Gilder to be your date to the wedding," I said. "Someone should be happy next Saturday. It might as well be you."

Catherine shook her head adamantly. "Going solo. Usually I skip the ceremony and show up for the reception, but I'm making an exception this time."

"Oh, why is that?"

"Because if you make a complete ass of yourself, I don't want to miss a second of it."

"Has anyone ever told you that you're a weird therapist?"

"All the time." Catherine leaned back in her chair and smiled proudly. "Thank you."

CHAPTER 14

I WAS SURPRISED to receive a message from Pansy to meet her at Larkspur Bridge where Walter's body was discovered. I wasn't surprised, however, that the message came via Elf Express rather than by owl. Apparently, Quinty was the original brains behind Elf Express, although he sold the company early on.

"Why do you think she wants to meet me without Astrid?" I asked.

Gareth hovered beside me, contemplating the message. "I suppose there's something she wants to tell you that she doesn't want the sheriff to know."

I swallowed hard. "That she killed him? Because I'm not exactly chomping at the bit to put myself in another dangerous situation." It seemed that I was always unknowingly putting myself in harm's way.

"I'd offer to go with you, but you know my skills aren't that advanced yet."

"*Yet* is the key word there," I said. "You're making tremendous strides, Gareth. You'll be haunting the whole town in no time."

"I don't want to haunt it," he said. "I just want to paint it red again."

I wrinkled my nose. "I don't think it's cool for a vampire to talk about painting the town red. It gives a violent impression."

He chuckled. "Fair enough. I only meant that I'd like to have fun again."

"According to Althea, you never had fun when you were able to go anywhere in town you liked. You were always busy with work."

"Exactly why it would be wonderful to ditch these chains and roam freely," he said. "I've learned from my mistakes. I want to play more and care less."

A lesson that came too late for too many people. Although Gareth wasn't quite getting a second chance, it was better than oblivion.

"Why does she want to meet at the bridge?" I asked aloud.

"Take Sedgwick with you," Garth advised. "That way if the elf is up to any shenanigans, you have backup."

"I'll bring my wand, too," I said. I plucked Tiffany from the glass jar on the kitchen counter.

He shook his head. "Only you would keep your wand in a biscuit jar."

"It's not a biscuit jar," I argued. "It's an open jar for nonspecific use. I can use it for anything I like. Things don't have to be so rigid, you know."

He sighed gently. "Yes, I'm beginning to learn."

I whistled loudly and Sedgwick came careening into the kitchen, nearly crashing into the window.

"I didn't actually expect you to respond so enthusiastically," I said. "Now that's progress."

I heard the word biscuit, Sedgwick said. *Don't get too excited.*

"I could say the same to you," I said. "There are no biscuits. We were only referencing the jar."

Sedgwick rolled his owl eyes. *False advertising. I demand reparations.*

"How about a nice mouse for lunch?"

How about twenty of them? Now where is it that I need to accompany you?

I smiled. "Oh, so you heard that part, too. I hadn't realized."

You talk. I listen. It's a problem. You're like a frequency I can't tune out.

I bit back a smile. "I'm sorry to inconvenience you. Did you have a nail appointment or something?"

Sedgwick scowled at me, as much as an owl was capable of scowling. *I was resting on my perch. Some of us like rest. We don't always need to be minding everyone else's business.*

I clutched my chest in mock indignation. "I didn't ask to meet Pansy. She asked to meet me. I can't help it if people want to talk to me."

People generally want to kill you, he said. *I guess that's where I come in.*

"You'd be very sad if something bad happened to me," I said. "Who would you have to harass then?"

That's true, he said grimly. *It would be a lonely road.*

"Are you going to drive Sigmund?" Gareth asked.

"I was actually thinking about riding my broom," I said.

Gareth staggered backward and instinctively gripped the wall behind him for support, even though he easily could have glided straight through it.

"Why would you do such a thing?" Gareth asked.

I drew breath. "Because I want to tackle my fears. Dr. Hall thinks it's important that I don't avoid things that make me uncomfortable."

"It makes you more than uncomfortable," he argued. "It makes you vomit. It's a health and safety issue."

"Yes, I know how concerned you are with health and

safety violations." When I first arrived in Spellbound, one of the first things I learned about Gareth was that he'd launched a petition to remove Holy water from the church due to health and safety issues for vampires.

"Let's go, Sedgwick," I said. "Pansy is probably already there waiting."

"Well, at least someone will be there as a witness if you drop out of the sky," Gareth said.

I took the broom out of the pantry and carried it out front. Sedgwick flew above me, offering his version of encouraging words.

Do your best not to die, he said.

"That's the plan," I said. "Aside from that, I'm not really sure what to expect."

You took your anti-anxiety potion this morning, I hope.

"I did. I think if I don't have to worry about keeping down my breakfast that I'll be able to focus on flying." I hoped anyway.

I swung one leg over the broom and said the magic words. "Take us off the grassy ground/to where birdsong is the only sound."

The broom began to rise and I resisted the urge to grip it tightly. I tried to keep calm so that my anxiety didn't spill over onto the broom. I was beginning to see how my energy affected things around me. I wobbled slightly in the air, tilting left and right before finding a sense of balance. I tried to channel Millie, even pretending that she was right behind me and actually flying the broom. I wanted to be better at this. I wanted to be better at everything. At living my life. I swore to myself that if Daniel snapped out of the spell, the first thing I would do is ask him how he felt about me. Of course, I'd already admitted my feelings, so maybe I would just be putting my feet in the fire to feel the burn. Regardless, I needed to be brave when it mattered most. Unlike vampires and ghosts, I only got one shot at my life. I had no interest in wasting it.

Where is this bridge? Sedgwick asked. We flew above Spellbound and, as always, I was mesmerized by its picturesque beauty. The clock tower. The church spire. The view from up here was inspiring. Although I certainly never dreamed of ending up in a place like this, I'd grown to love it in a very short time.

As we approached the part of the forest where the bridge was located, I began to slow my speed. Millie was much better at landings than I was. To be fair, Millie was much better at most things than I was. The trees were thicker and closer together than I anticipated and I found myself jerking the broom from side to side to avoid knocking into branches.

Steady now, Sedgwick called. *You look like you're riding a bucking centaur.*

I think I would actually be better at that, I replied.

A group of leaves smacked me in the face on the way down and a branch poked me in the eye. One hand let go of the broom to cover my eye and that was enough to send me into a tailspin. The broom circled and smacked into every branch it encountered on the way to the ground. I landed with a hard thud on the ground with my skirt yanked up over my head. Good thing I opted to wear underpants.

"Stars and stones, are you okay?" Pansy asked, rushing forward.

I sat up, dazed and confused. I pulled a few leaves from my hair. "I think so. Nothing to worry about. Just minor bruises."

And your sanity, Sedgwick added from above. He perched on a nearby branch to observe.

I yanked my skirt down and tried to regain my dignity. "So why did you want to meet here, Pansy?"

The petite elf glanced furtively around the forest, as

though someone might be listening. "I didn't want Astrid to hear what I'm about to tell you. Her sister is friends with my brother. I'd prefer that none of this makes it back to him."

"But Astrid is the sheriff," I said.

"Exactly," Pansy said. "Whatever I say to her becomes part of the official record. I want this kept quiet. Please." Her green eyes implored me. Whatever she had to say, she was desperate to keep it secret.

"Okay, I'll keep it to myself."

She breathed a sigh of relief. "Thank you. Can you walk? We need to head up this path over here."

I wouldn't have noticed the path if she hadn't pointed it out. With the overgrown bushes and other evidence of nature run amok, it wasn't obvious. I followed her through the brambles and thicket until we reached a small building no larger than a simple log cabin.

"What is this place?" I asked.

She beckoned me forward. "Come and see." She opened the wooden door and I followed her inside.

It was a much smaller version of Quinty's workshop. There were two tables covered in gizmos and gadgets.

"I don't understand," I said. "Is this another one of your brother's workshops?"

"No, this was Walter's place."

"Walter worked here, too?"

"He liked to tinker as much as Quinty," Pansy said. "But my brother is very territorial. He likes to be the main inventor. Walter had ideas that he wanted to try, but Quinty was calling all the shots. So Walter decided to set up a secret workshop of his own and have a couple of pet projects."

I walked over to inspect some of the materials. In a large, clear box hung a set of transparent wings. I had no doubt they belonged to Jeremiah's wife. Beside the box was a canister labeled 'pixie dust.' That was one problem solved.

"You're Quinty's sister," I said. "Why would he trust you with this information?" It was then that I noticed the personal space in the far corner of the room. A small dresser and a double bed. The troll was wide, but not so wide that he needed a double bed. Suddenly everything became painfully clear.

I glanced quickly at Pansy. "You two were having an affair?"

Her cheeks burned a fiery red. "I don't like the word affair. We were in love and had been for a long time."

"Wow," I breathed. I hadn't been expecting that confession. "Do you think his wife found out about you? Do you think it's possible that she killed him in anger?"

"I doubt it," Pansy said. "We were very careful and Marianne didn't take much interest in Walter's inventions." Her brow creased. "There was an incident near work one day, though, and it wasn't too long ago."

"With Marianne?"

Pansy shook her head and her ponytail swished from side to side. "No, her best friend. A fairy called Venla. She's a facialist over at Glow."

"What did she see?" I asked. If she got an eyeful, she may have run straight back to Marianne.

"Not much," Pansy admitted. "We were holding hands. Walter spotted her first and moved his hand away, but I'm not sure whether he was quick enough."

There was only one way to find out.

"Thank you for telling me the truth," I said. "I understand your reluctance to come forward, but if you were close to Walter, your information could lead to his killer."

Pansy sniffed. "I miss him terribly. I keep coming back here expecting to see him hunched over a project." She hugged her chest. "What's harder is not being able to grieve openly. He was the love of my life, but I'm expected to mourn him like a co-worker."

I didn't envy Pansy. It was a difficult situation.

"Did he love Marianne?" I asked.

"As a friend," Pansy said.

"Then why didn't he leave?" They didn't have children. There was nothing tying him to Marianne.

Pansy fiddled with a lever. "He thought she was too fragile. That a separation would break her."

I tapped the clear container with the pixie wings. "Do you know what he needed these for?"

Pansy's expression brightened. "His big project. He was sure this would be his breakthrough."

I glanced around at the disorganized table and tried to discern exactly what the project was. "What am I looking at?"

"A flying machine," Pansy replied and I detected a note of pride in her voice. "He wanted to invent a contraption that allowed non-magic users to fly around town the way you fly on your broomstick."

Like a magical jetpack. Impressive. "Was he successful?"

"On the verge," Pansy said. "He needed more money..." She trailed off and I sensed a story there.

"Where did he get the money to start it in the first place?"

She bit her lip, unsure whether to continue.

"Pansy," I said. "If you want to help catch Walter's killer, then I need to know everything you know, even if you think it's unrelated."

Pansy sighed. "Lord Gilder commissioned it."

My brow lifted. "Lord Gilder? Why?"

"He dabbles in a lot of ventures," Pansy said. "That was how the vampires started the blood bank co-op. It was Lord Gilder's idea."

Clever vampire. "Why did Walter need more funding?"

"I don't know the details," Pansy said. "Walter didn't want

to talk about it. They'd had a disagreement and Lord Gilder pulled the remainder of his funding."

A disagreement. Well, that was definitely a solid lead.

"Please don't tell him I'm the one who told you," Pansy said. "I don't want to be on his bad side." She shivered. "He frightens me."

"Really? I've found him to be delightful." Lorenzo Mancini, on the other hand, was another story.

Pansy gripped my arm, her eyes brimming with tears. "You won't tell anyone about me, will you? I don't want Marianne or Quinty to know."

"Are you sure you don't want to confide in your brother?" I asked. "It might help you grieve to share your good memories with someone else who knew him well."

Pansy shook her head. "It's my burden to bear. I won't saddle my brother with the weight of it."

I gave her a quick hug. "Don't worry. We'll find his killer."

"I believe you."

I released her and gestured to the wings and pixie dust. "Would you mind if I take these with me? I know someone who's missing them."

"Please do. The project is done now anyway." She glanced around the workshop, the sadness rolling off of her in waves.

"Are you coming?" I asked, heading for the door.

"I think I'll stay here for a while longer," she said.

I nodded and left her alone with her thoughts.

CHAPTER 15

ON THE WAY to my office, I noticed a crowd gathered in front of the Great Hall. A few signs waved in the air and I tried to get a good look at the messages. *Freedom to Pee* was written on one in bright yellow paint. I was pretty sure the drips were intentional. Another one read *Shift Free or Die*. So this was a shifter protest. As I drew closer, I heard the chant of 'the Buck stops here.'

Oh no. They were protesting the charges against Buck. This was the last thing I needed. I elbowed my way through the crowd until I located a familiar face.

"Alex," I exclaimed. "I thought you were going to do this through the proper channels."

Alex gave me a regretful look. "The mayor refused to put us on the calendar for the council meeting. We didn't feel like we had a choice. If they refuse to hear our voices through official channels, then this is the only option."

I surveyed the chanting shifters. At least it was a peaceful protest. For now.

"Is anyone even in the Great Hall right now?" I asked. If not, the protest was like a tree falling in the woods.

"Not right now," Alex admitted. "But we're getting the attention of the community. Plenty of residents are passing by and wanting to know what the protest is about."

"It's all about drawing attention to the cause," Patsy said.

"Listen, I'm on your side," I said. "I just feel like there's a lot going on in town right now and sometimes timing is crucial to success."

"Easy for you to say when you can be yourself all day every day," Patsy sneered.

"Yeah, and you can pee anywhere you like," another werewolf said.

I frowned. "Well, that's not entirely true." Because I had the bladder of a woman pregnant with triplets, I had to make sure I was aware of the nearest bathroom at all times. That was how I coped.

"I've got the urge to urinate right now," a werewolf said and began to unzip his jeans.

Alex placed a firm hand on his shoulder. "Let's keep this civil, Franklin. No need to rile people up. We want them to support us, not be disgusted by us."

"You callin' your own kind disgusting?" Franklin shot back.

Alex put his face an inch from Franklin's. "You know perfectly well that's not what I'm saying. If you have a problem with me, then you can take it up at the next pack meeting."

Franklin quickly backed down. "'Course not. Tensions are running high is all."

"That minotaur is walking around with his horns on display, but we still can't shift in the middle of the day," LuAnn said. "It's discrimination."

The shifters had a point. On the other hand, Markos in minotaur form was more of a hybrid. When a werewolf shifted to a wolf, there was no human element left. It was a full shift to an animal form.

"Where's Buck?" I asked, glancing at the sea of faces.

"I told him to stay behind," Alex said. "I didn't want to do anything that would hurt his case."

"I thank you for that, Alex," I said. I didn't need anything to make my job more difficult, especially now with so many other distractions.

Noise erupted from the far side of the crowd and Alex and I moved over to investigate.

"Why should we disperse?" Patsy demanded.

"This is a peaceful protest," another voice said. "We have every right to be here."

"According to regulation 5631-42, you need a permit." I recognized the voice of Stan, the town registrar.

"Did anyone apply for a permit?" a female voice yelled.

Shouts of 'no' echoed back at her.

Stan bowed his head. "Then I'm afraid you need to break up this party. I'm sorry. Rules are rules."

I closed my eyes and heaved a disappointed sigh. Spellbound was far too reliant on rules and regulations. Making them disperse was only going to increase their irritability.

Franklin shoved his way through the crowd and stood in front of Stan. "Well now, I'm going to leave you with a mark of my dissatisfaction." He unzipped his trousers and relieved himself. The urine streamed to the ground, forming a puddle at the edge of Stan's shoes.

To his credit, Stan didn't react. Instead, he glanced at me and said, "You and I were never here."

"Never where?" I said, stepping away from the crowd.

I heard Alex behind me, calling for the pack to listen and follow orders. It was like trying to herd cats…or werewolves.

· · ·

I made an appointment at Glow for the next day. My first fairy facial. I had no idea what to expect, especially considering I'd never had a facial in the human world. Extras like that were not in my budget. I also wasn't convinced that a facial was beneficial for anything other than your self-esteem. There was no science to suggest it actually helped your skin.

I turned up at Glow at eleven o'clock on the dot. I made sure to keep my face pure. No makeup or moisturizer. I couldn't help but look around in wonder at the sparkling interior of the salon. The enchanted salon tools never ceased to amaze me.

A fairy hovered by the reception desk, a lemon yellow wand in her hand.

"I'm here to see Venla," I said. "I have an appointment for a facial."

"Great! She'll be with you in a moment."

Two minutes later a fairy fluttered in from a back room. She smiled at the sight of me.

"You must be my eleven o'clock," Venla said. "Come on back."

I followed the fairy to a stylish yet comfortable room at the back of the salon. She patted the cushioned table.

"Make yourself comfortable," she said. "Put your head here and make sure you're facing up."

"Well, I'd be mighty impressed if you managed to do it with my face down."

"Have you decided which facial you'll be having today?" Venla asked.

"I've never had a facial before, so I don't know," I said. "What are my choices?"

Venla's wings ground to a halt. "You've never had a facial?"

"No, I was both time poor and cash poor in the human world."

Venla's eyes widened. "Oh, you're Emma Hart."

"Yes, your eleven o'clock."

Venla fluttered closer to me and began to inspect my face. "In that case, let me take a look at your skin and I'll let you know which facial I recommend." She produced a mirror seemingly from out of nowhere and held it up to my face. I instinctively shrank away. Every feature on my face looked enormous. My eyelashes looked like black licorice and my pores looked large enough to walk a camel through them.

"Stars and stones," I said, closing my eyes. "Does it have to be so close?"

"I'm just having a closer look at your skin type. It's very dry. Do you moisturize?"

"Every morning," I said.

"Not in the evening? After you've washed your face?"

"Should I?"

"If you want to have this beautiful skin in twenty more years, then I highly recommend it." She continued to scrutinize my skin. "A few wrinkles, but nothing to worry about at this stage."

A slow panic began to build. "A few wrinkles?"

"Like I said, nothing to worry about at this stage. You're still young. If you take good care of your skin from here on out, you'll have no problems."

"I have to worry about my skin, too?" I already felt the weight of the world on my shoulders. I didn't really want to add crypt keeper skin to the long list of things to panic about.

"I recommend either the fizz whiz facial or the sparkle-berry infusion," Venla said.

"I have no idea what either one of those entails, but I'll leave it to your professional judgment."

Venla tapped her perfectly manicured nail on her chin. "I'm going to go with sparkleberry infusion. Get that healthy glow back in your cheeks."

"A healthy glow sounds good," I said.

Venla began to gather her materials in preparation for the facial. I watched as she used her wand and gently tapped each item.

"Do you use fairy magic for the facial?" I asked.

She glanced at me over her shoulder. "Of course. This is a fairy salon. What else would we use?"

I had no clue. "You seem close in age to Elsa Knightsbridge. Did you go to school together?"

Venla scowled. "We did, not that she would acknowledge my existence. I tended not to hang out with other fairies."

A-ha. There was my opening. "Who did you hang out with?"

"My best friend is a troll. You can imagine how well that went over in the fairy community, especially in high school. Trolls are inelegant creatures, not really our type, if you know what I mean."

"All of the trolls I've met here have been wonderful," I said. That was true.

"Marianne and I met in high school and we've been best friends ever since." She brought over a jar of multicolored sparkles that looked like confetti. She used an applicator and applied it to my face like a paste. "She's going through a tough time right now, in fact. Her husband died."

I watched her carefully out of the corner of my eye, praying she didn't douse my eyeball with sparkles. "That's terrible. What happened?"

Venla shrugged. "The sheriff is still investigating. Marianne is distraught, as you can imagine. Walter was her world." There was something in her tone that suggested he shouldn't have been.

"Did you like Walter? I imagine it would be hard if you don't like the husband of your best friend."

Venla continued to smear the paste across my cheeks. "I liked him well enough. I just don't think he was the troll she believed him to be."

"What makes you say that?"

Venla pressed her lips together. "Let's just say I found out some unflattering information about him recently. It made me angry."

"Did you tell Marianne about it?"

"No, because I didn't want to ruin our friendship. I felt like it would be one of those situations where the messenger might get the blame."

I understood her fear. Often times the person who didn't want to know the truth blamed the person who opened their eyes in the first place. It was a touchy situation.

"So this unflattering information," I began. "Are you going to tell her now that he's dead?"

"Absolutely not," she said emphatically. "What's the point? I would rather preserve her positive impression of him. Why sully his good name now? It's pointless. It seems to me that both women are suffering enough without him."

"Both women?" I repeated. So she did know about Pansy. I suspected as much, but I wasn't one hundred percent sure until now.

Venla heaved a sigh. "Yes. Walter had a mistress. I found out about it not that long ago when I saw them together near Walter's office. I was heartbroken for Marianne."

"Did you confront him?" I asked. She smoothed the paste so close to my lips that I was having trouble speaking at this point.

"No, but I know they saw me. I kept waiting for Walter to come and speak to me about it, but he never did."

"You said you were angry. Why didn't you go to see him about it?"

"Honestly, I was still deciding how to handle it. Marianne didn't seem unhappy with him and he treated her well. Part of me wondered whether she knew and chose to turn a blind eye."

That was an interesting theory. "Do you know how Walter died?"

"I heard he was found frozen to death in the woods," she said. "Some kind of magic spell."

"Fairy magic?" I queried.

"I certainly hope not," Venla said. "That would be bad for all of us."

"How's Marianne holding up?"

"She has good days and bad days," Venla said. "I've been trying to spend as much time with her as possible. She wants to reminisce about Walter. I find that a little difficult, but I indulge her."

"You don't think you'll ever tell her the truth?"

"No," she said firmly. "Her good memories of him are all she has left now. What kind of friend would I be if I destroyed that?"

"Were you around when Walter's body was found?" I asked. "Were you able to be with Marianne?"

"I was actually here when the message came," she replied. "I had the early shift, but my boss let me leave in the middle of a facial so that I could be there for Marianne. She knows how close we are."

There was no way that Venla killed Walter. Yes, she was a protective friend, but she never would have killed Walter over his affair. Not when she knew how much Marianne would suffer as a result. Plus she had an alibi as well. I was definitely ruling her out.

Venla fluttered back to admire her handiwork. "We're going to leave this mask on for twenty minutes. How does it feel?"

"Like someone vomited glitter all over my face," I said.

She smiled. "Perfect."

CHAPTER 16

VENLA'S WORDS stayed with me. What if Marianne knew the truth, but chose to turn a blind eye only to change her mind in the heat of the moment? It was a careful line to tread because if she didn't know, then I didn't want to be the one to tell her. I had to make sure that the conversation was vague enough to get a sense of her awareness without showing my hand.

I stopped outside Brew-Ha-Ha. I waited until she retrieved her coffee from the counter to enter the coffee shop. I made sure to brush past her, pretending not to notice her. Basically, the way I was treated in high school.

"Miss Hart," she greeted me.

I broke my stride and turned toward her. "Mrs. Rivers," I said, feigning surprise. "Oh my goodness, how are you?"

"Please call me Marianne. I'm hanging in there," she said. "We had a lovely service for Walter. You should've seen it. So many friends came to say goodbye." Her eyes glistened with tears. "I was really touched to see the outpouring of love for him."

"I assume everyone was there from work," I said.

"Oh yes. Quinty was there. And his sister, Pansy. They've known Walter forever and a day." She glanced around the room. "Would you like to join me for a few minutes? Grab a drink and come sit down."

I smiled. "Don't mind if I do. I hate to drink alone."

That was true. Although I didn't consider myself an introvert, I didn't like eating alone in restaurants either. It was plain boring.

I hurried to the counter and placed my order. Henrik greeted me with his usual snarl. I knew better than to be intimidated by it. It was part of the berserker's charm.

"Thanks, Henrik," I said, as he handed me my latte with a boost of sunshine. I joined Marianne at the table by the window.

"How are you handling things?" I asked. "One day at a time?" That was how I coped.

She nodded and sipped her drink. "I'm trying to force myself to leave the house. That's why I'm here now. If I don't force myself, then I'm prone to sit in the house and cry. That's not the life Walter would want for me."

No, certainly not. Much like I knew my parents wouldn't want me to live a life of no loving relationships because I feared their loss.

"You showered and left the house," I said. "That's a huge win."

She gave me an appreciative smile. "Thank you. I think so too."

"I'm sure you gave a lovely speech at his service," I said. I wondered whether Pansy had cried throughout the service and, if so, whether Marianne had noticed.

"I didn't think I would manage to get through the speech," Marianne said. "Walter would have been proud of me. Public speaking was never my thing. He was the gregarious one."

I patted her arm. "You give him all the credit, Marianne.

You seem to have no shortage of friends."

She took another sip and set down her cup. "That's true. I'm very grateful for them, especially Venla. I don't know what I'd do without her."

"You and Walter seemed to have a wonderful friendship on top of everything else," I said. "You probably didn't feel the need for too many friends when you have a husband like that."

"I suppose," she said. "But he did spend a lot of time on his inventions. If I didn't have other friends, I would have been very lonely."

"An invention widow," I said. In the human world, some wives were called football widows during the NFL season. It was probably much the same for Marianne.

"And now an actual widow," she said sadly.

My hand whipped across my mouth. "Oh, Marianne. How thoughtless of me. I'm so sorry."

"Don't be," she said. "I know I'm romanticizing our relationship now that he's dead. Of course he wasn't perfect. No relationship is perfect."

"Was that your main issue with him?" I asked, careful not to push too hard. "Did you argue about the time he spent on inventions?"

"Pretty much," she said. "It seemed like all his free time was spent on perfecting them. That left little time for me. It seemed to get worse over the last few years or so. I often thought about leaving him, but I didn't want to do that to him. I don't think he could have managed without me."

Oh, the cruel irony. I resisted the urge to comment. Instead I asked, "Why do you think he was so obsessed with the inventions?"

She settled back in her chair, thinking. "I don't really know. Some days I felt like he was bored with me. We would be sitting together and he would get this faraway look in his eyes.

I knew he was somewhere else in his head." Her expression softened. "It annoyed me a bit, but I never asked him about it."

"Why not?"

"I don't know. Part of me probably didn't want to know the answer."

"Do you think he was happy with you?" A potentially incendiary question.

"I don't really know what happy is. We liked each other well enough. We never fought. I suppose that's a kind of happiness."

There was no way Marianne knew about Pansy. She may have suspected something, but she preferred to hide her head in the sand than discover the truth. She wanted her rose-colored version of events to be the final word on her marriage. Part of me understood.

"You're still young, Marianne. I don't mean to speak too soon, but maybe in a year or so you'll be ready to start a new relationship."

Marianne burst into laughter. "I don't know that anyone would have an old troll like me, but thank you for the suggestion."

I shrugged. "There's always Pandora. People seem happy with her matchmaking service."

The door to the coffee shop opened and Hugo strode in, his hooves leaving scuffmarks on the floor. He growled when he saw me.

"Meddling again, Hart?"

I shot him an innocent look. "I don't know what you mean. Marianne and I are having a friendly chat over lattes. You should try it sometime."

"If you need someone to help you figure out what happened to your husband," he said to Marianne, "don't hesitate to call a professional."

"She has a professional," I said. "Sheriff Astrid is going to crack this case wide open any day now."

"Thank you for the offer," Marianne said. "But I have confidence in the sheriff. She's been keeping me updated on the case and she is committed to finding Walter's killer."

Hugo blew a short puff of air from his nostrils and stalked off toward the counter.

"Talk about someone who needs a hobby," Marianne said, and I laughed.

"Did you mean it?" I asked. "Are you satisfied with Sheriff Astrid's performance so far?" I didn't want to assume that everyone was happy with her. I knew that I tended to be loyal to a fault.

"Solving a murder isn't magic," Marianne said. "It takes time. I know that. She's doing her best and I have confidence that she'll bring the murderer to justice."

"She'll be happy to hear that," I said. "I'm sure not everyone would have your patience."

Marianne drained her cup and stared out the window. "If that was one thing Walter taught me, it was patience. You don't learn how to wait for someone day after day without learning a thing or two about it."

Yes, I wholeheartedly agreed. When you were forced to live according to someone else's timetable, patience was the only option.

"Emma, it's good to see you."

"Hi, Paisley," I greeted the witch. Paisley was unlucky enough to work alongside Jemima at Mix-n-Match. "I brought a friend tonight. I hope no one minds."

Paisley smiled at Britta. "It's harp therapy. No one minds anything. We're all too relaxed."

"And you swear this is better than knitting?" Britta asked, clearly unconvinced.

"It is for me," I said. "The only way to know for sure is to try it."

Britta surveyed the room full of harps. "Looks like a bunch of old timers."

"Watch who you're calling old, Viking." Phoebe Minor swept past us and took her seat next to Sheena Stone.

"Whoa," Britta breathed. "You've got a harpy in here. That's hardcore."

I smiled. "I think that's the first time anyone has referred to harp therapy as hardcore." I spotted two empty seats together and guided her over. "Maybe spend the first half of the class listening."

Britta apparently wasn't very good at listening. She plopped down in the chair and immediately began to pluck the strings. With her tongue.

"Sounds weird," she said.

"The way you're doing it, yes, it does," Phoebe said.

Britta's expression shifted and she gave the harpy the calm, cold look of death. Uh oh.

"Britta," I said, gently removing her face from the harp. "Maybe listen and learn. The sound of the harp can be very soothing."

"I'm not sure it's really my style," Britta said. "I like loud, thumping music." She hopped to her feet and jumped around in a small circle, jerking her head back and forth.

"Is she having a seizure?" Phoebe asked. "Quick, someone whip up an anti-seizure tonic."

Britta continued to demonstrate her dance moves, unperturbed.

"She's dancing to the beat of her own drum," I said.

"There aren't any drums here," an elderly voice interjected.

"Not literal drums, Melvin," Phoebe snapped. "Put in your hearing aid."

"I heard her fine," Melvin objected. "I just misunderstood is all." He plucked a few strings. "Harpy."

"Damn straight," Phoebe shot back. "Faun."

"How about we stop the name calling?" I suggested. They were worse than the town council as children.

"She *is* a harpy," Melvin said.

"And he *is* a faun," Phoebe replied, her voice bristling with irritation.

"Then maybe stop saying the words with such disdain," I suggested. "There's nothing wrong with being a harpy or a faun. They're both lovely."

"Well," Britta began. "I don't know that I'd call a harpy *lovely*. That's a bit of a stretch."

The harp music came to a screeching halt and everyone stared at Britta. There was a collective uneasy pause.

"Oh no?" Phoebe asked. "And how exactly would you describe a harpy?"

Britta shrugged, seemingly unaware of the venom in Phoebe's tone. I began to wonder whether Britta had a death wish.

"Tough old birds?"

Phoebe seemed satisfied with her response. "Fair enough."

"Have a seat, Britta," I urged. "Class isn't long, so let's take advantage of it."

I began to strum the harp strings. Although I wasn't nearly as good as everyone else, the sound still managed to be pleasant.

"What song is that?" Britta asked.

"It's not a specific song," I said. "I'm just playing by ear."

"She's got the hang of it," Britta said, pointing to Sheena. "I could listen to that at bedtime. Might be a decent replacement for alcohol."

"You...drink alcohol so you can sleep?" I queried.

"It helps."

Sometimes it was hard to believe that Astrid and Britta were sisters. As similar as they looked, their personalities were night and day.

"Why do you have trouble getting to sleep?" I asked, thinking of my own anxiety.

"My dreams suck," Britta admitted. "Some nights I don't want to sleep so I can avoid them. When I drink enough, I don't remember my dreams."

Wow. That seemed to be a horrible way to live.

"What kind of dreams?" Phoebe asked. She seemed genuinely interested, which was uncharacteristic of the aging harpy.

Britta inhaled deeply. "Battlefield stuff. Lots of blood and gore. Missing limbs. I know I'm supposed to be cool with that because I'm a Viking badass, but it freaks me out."

"Why do you think you dream about it?" I asked. "It's not like you're fighting any battles here. Spellbound is fairly quiet." Except for the occasional murder.

"It's in my blood," Britta said. "My brother has them too, but he enjoys them."

"What about Astrid?" I asked.

"She doesn't seem to mind them," Britta said. "When I ask her, she says she barely remembers her dreams."

The sounds of the harp lulled me into a sleepy state of mind as I focused on my music. Razor-like snoring erupted beside me and I noticed Britta's head tilted back. A long trail of drool dripped down her cheek and onto the floor.

"I guess harp music relaxes her after all," Sheena remarked.

I studied the Valkyrie. "I hate to wake her." Not only because she appeared peaceful, but also because she struck me as someone who might attack upon waking.

"Pretty," Britta breathed between snores.

"What'd she say?" Phoebe asked.

"Pretty dress," Britta said. "I like roses."

"She likes roses," Melvin said loudly.

"Fire is pretty too," a sleeping Britta added.

Um, okay. Apparently not the battlefield dream she was worried about.

"She likes fire," Melvin said, trying to be our helpful interpreter.

"Thanks, Melvin," Phoebe said. "We got it."

"Class is over," Sheena said, watching everyone pack up to leave. "Who wants to be the one to wake her?"

"Emma should do it," Melvin said. "She's the one who brought her." I didn't miss his accusatory tone.

"I don't have a weapon," I objected.

"Oh, for Nature's sake, I'll do it," Phoebe said, rising to her feet. As she reached to shake Britta's shoulder, the Valkyrie's eyes popped open and she shot up out of her seat. Britta grabbed the harpy's arm, twisting it backward.

"Ouch," Phoebe cried. "Let go of me, you demented Viking. I have brittle bird bones."

Britta released her grip on the harpy and blinked. "Did I fall asleep?"

Phoebe rubbed her arm. "You snore like a pirate. Trust me, I know what that sounds like." She shuddered. "I miss the hulk of a man, but not the snoring."

"I fell asleep?" Britta repeated. "In the daytime? Like a nap?"

"Technically, it's evening," Sheena said. "But yes, dear. You fell asleep."

Britta stretched her arms over her head and grinned like a lunatic. "I took a nap and my dreams were pleasant. No bloodshed. That's incredible." She clapped me hard between the shoulder blades. "Thanks, Emma. This has been great. How often does this class meet?"

"Twice a week," I said.

Britta nodded. "Awesome. It's going on my calendar."

"You want to come here so you can nap?" Phoebe queried.

"You want to come here so you can gripe about people," Britta said. "Why is my reason any worse?"

Phoebe regarded the deputy with a newfound respect. "Welcome to harp therapy, Valkyrie."

"I don't know how I'm going from this to a raging nightclub later," Paisley commented. "I should really reverse the order."

"Big night out?" I asked.

"Usually we go to Olympus, but I heard Elsa's having her bachelorette party there tonight, so we're going to Decadence instead."

I perked up at the mention of the bachelorette party. "I haven't heard of Olympus," I said.

"You haven't been there yet?" Paisley asked, stunned. "It's the nightclub where all the young people hang out. I would have thought your friends would've taken you there by now."

"To be honest, they're not really the nightclub types." But Gareth was. I'd have to see if Olympus was one of the places he liked to frequent before his death.

"When you say young people," Phoebe began, "you mean hot slabs of man meat, right?"

Paisley nodded. "Definitely young hot guys. They seem to flock there. That's probably why Elsa chose it for her bachelorette party. She likes the attention."

No doubt.

"This is a party for Elsa to let loose and go nuts before her lifetime commitment," Melvin said. "When you live as long as most of us do, a lifetime commitment is a scary prospect."

Not for me. If I lived a million years, Daniel was still the one I wanted by my side. The gears began turning in my mind. Since I failed to find the right Anti-Obsession potion, maybe I could use the bachelorette party to gather evidence of Elsa having a little too much fun at Olympus. Would Daniel be upset enough to call off the wedding? If I couldn't fight the Obsession potion, then maybe I could work with it instead. Exploit his obsession.

"What's the dress code for Olympus?" I asked.

Paisley cocked an eyebrow. "Are you sure this is a good idea?"

"Of course not," I said. "But that never seems to serve as a roadblock."

"Okay then. The less material on your body, the better," Paisley said. "I think maybe I should go with you and make sure things don't get out of hand. I wouldn't want the coven to have any issues with the fairies as a result of your exploits."

"Exploits?" I asked, blinking innocently. "I have no interest in exploits of my own." Only Elsa's.

"You go to Decadence. I'll pick Emma up at eight," Phoebe Minor interjected.

Paisley laughed. "It doesn't even open that early."

Phoebe's brow furrowed. "Eight o'clock is early? When did that happen?"

"When you got old," Sheena said. "I want to come too. I haven't been to a nightclub in ages."

I smacked my forehead. "I don't know. You two tend to wreak havoc when you go out drinking."

Phoebe and Sheena high-fived each other.

"Damn straight," Phoebe said. "And I've got the perfect outfit in mind. It's hanging in Calliope's closet right now."

My stomach churned. The less material, the better? Somehow I doubted that this would be the bachelorette party that Elsa had envisioned for herself.

CHAPTER 17

"YOU CANNOT POSSIBLY EXPECT to show up at Olympus wearing that," Gareth said, scrutinizing me.

I glanced down at the faux leather skirt and sparkly halter top. "What's wrong with this?" It seemed right up his alley. I looked like a combination of his disco ball and his own pair of leather trousers hidden in his closet.

"You need to show as much flesh as possible. This covers all the good stuff." Magpie hopped up on the bed and hissed in agreement.

"Well, I'm not going to show up naked," I objected.

"You want to blend, don't you?"

My eyes bulged. "People don't actually turn up naked, do they?" Because that was out of the question. Not to mention Elsa seemed far too uptight for that kind of thing.

"A gallon of body glitter would do the trick," Gareth said.

"A gallon? How big do you think I am?" I folded my arms. "Forget it. I'm not demeaning myself in front of Elsa."

Gareth clucked his tongue. "You're showing up at her bachelorette party to try and weasel her fiancé out from under her. I'd say you're demeaning yourself just fine without the glitter."

"I'm not wearing body glitter, but I don't have the type of outfit you think I need."

The sound of wind chimes interrupted us. Gareth inclined his head. "Your ride is early."

"Very." Phoebe wasn't due for another half an hour. "See who it is."

Gareth returned a moment later. "It's Phoebe Minor all right. I'd recognize that scowl anywhere. And she's come bearing gifts."

I raced to the front door. Sure enough, Phoebe stood on the front porch, her arm draped with clothes.

"Phoebe, do you need help choosing an outfit?" I asked.

"No, dimwit. I'm here to help you. I already look awesome." She brushed past me and thrust a pile of clothes into my arms. "Now hurry up. We don't want to stand at the end of the line. My arthritic hip will start acting up."

I took one look at her outfit and my eyes widened. I'd never seen so much wrinkled cleavage in my life. It looked like two Shar-Peis fighting under a blanket.

"You look so…youthful," I said.

"That's the goal," she replied. "Now you need to change out of those schoolmarm clothes and find something suitable in here."

I held up a shiny rainbow tube top. "Where did you get these?"

"The vintage closet in the attic," she said. "Everything comes back in style eventually so we keep it all. When you have six harpies under one roof, you tend to have a lot of clothes." She yanked the remnants of a dress from my arm. "Try this."

I stared at the flimsy fabric. The silver dress was thigh-high and sheer with cutouts in the abdominal area and the back.

"You've absolutely got to wear that," Gareth said, floating downstairs.

"Are you serious?"

"As an enchantress with a grudge," Phoebe said, mistakenly thinking my response was to her. "Don't be shy. You've got the body for this."

I glanced down at myself. "I guess I can try it on."

"Hurry up. I'm thirsty."

"I have plenty to drink here," I said.

"For booze, you silly witch. Now get changed and let's go."

"She's feisty," Gareth said with an air of approval. "If Elsa gives you any trouble, just toss Phoebe between you. That'll nip it in the bud."

I hoped it didn't come to that. I wanted to fly below the radar and dig for dirt. Before Phoebe could snarl at me again, I carried the so-called dress upstairs to get changed. Daniel had no clue the lengths I was willing to go to for him. Maybe someday he'd have the chance to appreciate it.

The club was jam-packed. I'd never seen so many wings and horns in one place since my arrival in Spellbound. And here I thought I'd met every attractive member of the community. It seemed that a large portion of them were hiding out at nightclubs like Olympus.

Phoebe made a beeline for the bar where Sheena awaited her and I located Begonia cowering near the restrooms.

Begonia gripped my arm nervously. "Where did all these good-looking paranormals come from?"

I gave her a curious look. "You're just as pretty as any of these girls. You know that, right?"

She nudged me with her elbow. "You're such a good friend. Anyway, it isn't that," she said, hesitating. "Claude and I have been getting along really well. Looking around here makes me question my willingness to commit though."

"You're still young, Begonia. You don't have to make big decisions like that yet, unless you're absolutely sure."

"I'm sure that Claude is lovely and we have a great time together," she admitted.

"But you're not sure if you see him sticking around long-term?"

"Oh, I think *he* would stick around. I'm not sure whether I would. To be honest, I haven't given it much thought."

"Don't stress about it. You're not here tonight to find a new boyfriend anyway. We're here to keep an eye on Elsa and see if we can get any information that stops the wedding."

Begonia surveyed the crowd. "There are so many bodies crammed in the room. She won't even know we're here."

I felt a sharp tap on my shoulder and craned my neck to see who was behind me.

"Who had the poor taste to invite you to my bachelorette party?" Elsa stood behind me, her arms folded, accentuating her ample cleavage. She looked ready for nightclub action with her hair pulled up in a high ponytail and her exposed skin dusted with golden glitter.

"It's not a closed event," I said. "The nightclub is open to the public in case you haven't noticed."

Elsa glared at me. "It just so happens that I'm good friends with the owner's daughter. Watch your step or I'll have you thrown out of here and humiliated."

"What will you do? Slip a potion into my drink?" I challenged her.

Her blue eyes narrowed. "Stay out of my way, witch." She elbowed me hard as she passed by and her friends sashayed behind her, looking exactly like the mean girls they were.

"Maybe we should leave," Begonia suggested. "I don't want her making trouble for you."

"Are you nuts?" I asked. "Now I'm more determined than ever to stick around and see what she gets up to. I don't trust her for a second."

"Do you really think she'll step far enough out of line that Daniel will change his mind about the wedding?"

I pondered the question. "I don't know, but it's my last chance, Begonia. I have to try."

She nodded mutely.

"Emma Hart. I don't think I've ever seen you look as delicious as you do right now."

I turned to see Demetrius beside me. "You'd better be careful, Dem. The last thing you want is to tell a human she looks delicious."

He laughed softly. "I do appreciate your sense of humor. It's one of your most attractive qualities."

"I didn't realize you frequented the nightclubs."

"I like to dance." He paused, his gaze traveling over my sheer silver not-quite-a-dress. "A pity we never got that far."

"Begonia likes to dance," I said, nudging her forward.

Begonia's cheeks burned scarlet. "I…do."

His fangs popped out at the sight of Begonia's deep V-neck top. I didn't blame him. I'd never seen Begonia look sexy before. Her nightclub outfit was the equivalent of Sandy's transformation from ponytailed sweetheart to leather-clad hot girl in *Grease*.

"There's a good song playing right now," Demetrius said, extending a hand toward her.

Begonia cast a wary look at me and I waved her off. She'd had a crush on Demetrius forever. There was no way I'd discourage her.

"I'll be fine," I insisted. "Plenty here to keep me occupied." Like keeping track of Elsa.

"If you're sure," Begonia said.

I gave her a gentle push toward Demetrius and I watched until they were swallowed by the pulsating crowd on the dance floor.

Poor Claude. He didn't stand a chance against the charms of Demetrius Hunt.

I scanned the club for any sign of Elsa and her friends. Her location wasn't difficult to pinpoint. I saw her perched on the balcony of the second floor, prancing around like she owned the place. Her friends mimicked her actions, copying her every gyration. It was nauseating to watch. If I didn't stop this wedding, Daniel was going to marry the Ultimate Mean Girl. Ugh.

Someone bumped into me, spilling liquid all over my legs and feet. The apology barely registered. I was fixated on Elsa, determined not to miss a single piece of damnable evidence.

"Most people come here to drink and dance," a voice said. "You don't seem to be doing either one."

"Huh?" I glanced over to see a heart-stoppingly handsome man. Wavy, brown hair and celadon eyes. Broad shoulders and a body with more definitions than the dictionary. No sign of horns, wings, or a tail though. When he grinned, I immediately developed a new appreciation for the term 'instant panty remover.'

"You're an incubus," I said, the realization hitting me.

"And you're very pretty," he replied.

The sexual vibes surrounded him in a haze, threatening to drown me in a sea of pheromones. "Emma."

"Jackson." He inclined his head toward the dance floor. "Care to join me?"

Holy Hotness. How did anyone turn down his advances? It felt like a superpower. "I'd love to, but I can't."

He blinked, the words not quite registering. "Sorry?"

"I'm here on a mission and that doesn't include dancing, even with someone as tempting as you."

The compliment seemed to placate him. "My loss. If you change your mind, I'll be out there, bumping and grinding all by my lonesome."

I had a feeling he wouldn't be all by his lonesome for more than two seconds. Jackson seemed like a black hole of sex—he sucked you in and swallowed you whole.

His attention was suddenly drawn to the second floor, where Elsa was swinging around a pole and laughing.

"Elsa Knightsbridge," he said.

"It's her bachelorette party," I said.

"Is that right?" He flashed a crooked grin.

"You haven't heard about the wedding?" I queried. I figured everyone in town knew about Daniel and Elsa.

"Oh, I've heard, but I'm less interested in weddings than I am in bachelorette parties." He winked at me. "If you'll excuse me, it's my turn to make a bride-to-be blush."

A perfect storm was brewing and I had no way of capturing the moment. I didn't miss my cell phone often, but my phone camera would have come in very handy right now. A nice video of Elsa coiled around Mr. Sex On A Stick.

My dream died before Jackson made it to the bachelorette. Phoebe Minor intercepted him, her long, bony arms wrapping around his muscular frame. To his credit, he didn't shudder.

"Phoebe," I whispered. "You're supposed to be on my team."

I watched as the older harpy encouraged the incubus to dance with her. He humored her without so much as a backward glance at Elsa. He was either a gentlemanly incubus or he truly didn't care as long as he had a female body to rub against.

128

"We finally got in," Sophie said, squeezing my shoulders.

"Hey." I twisted my neck to greet Millie and Sophie. "You were in the line all that time?"

"We apparently aren't scantily clad enough," Millie said. "The bouncers kept letting mostly naked people in ahead of us."

She wasn't wrong. Both Millie and Sophie wore normal dresses—cute for a party but not on trend for Olympus.

"This place is super popular," Sophie said.

Millie seemed disinterested in the ambience. "Where's Elsa and what's the plan?"

"I want to catch her doing something inappropriate," I said. "Then Daniel will get so upset that he cancels the wedding."

Millie frowned. "How will you prove it?"

I bit my lip. "Not sure. Magic?"

"Where's Begonia?" Sophie asked.

"Dancing with Demetrius Hunt," I replied.

Sophie's eyes grew round. "Seriously? That's been her dream forever."

"Well, it's coming true right now, while I'm standing on the threshold of a nightmare." Not that I begrudged Begonia her happiness. I wanted everyone I cared about to find happiness. Otherwise, what was the point of living?

"There's someone who may help you," Millie said, pointing across the crowded room. Jasper, Elsa's former fiancé, pushed his way through the partygoers toward the spiral staircase that led to the second floor.

"He's heading straight for Elsa," Sophie said.

"What do you think he's going to do?" Millie asked. "She's already publicly humiliated him by dumping him for Daniel. He's nuts to pursue her now."

"He loves her," I said simply. "He's willing to endure anything she throws at him."

"He should have some self-respect," Millie snapped, oblivious to my similar situation.

I watched with interest, hoping to see her kiss him, or at the very least, flirt heavily. Unfortunately, I only witnessed her reject him all over again. Although I couldn't hear her actual words, I got the gist of them based on Jasper's crestfallen expression. He seemed confident that he could win her over. Poor Jasper. I empathized.

"That was a bust," Millie observed.

I sighed deeply. "I don't think we're going to catch Elsa doing anything in public. She's not that stupid." Unfortunately for me. Why couldn't she channel her intelligence into a worthwhile project like animal rescue?

"We should go now," I said, feeling dejected. "This is a waste of time."

"But we just got in," Millie objected.

"I'm sorry. Feel free to stay. You don't need to leave because I'm leaving."

"I'll come with you," Sophie volunteered. "This isn't my scene anyway. I only came to be supportive."

Millie chewed her lip, debating. "I think I'll stay, but I'll do you this one favor."

"What's that?" I asked.

Millie produced her wand and pointed it at Elsa. "From the wand of a witch/make the bitch itch."

My eyes widened as I watched Elsa begin to scratch herself. First her arm and then everywhere she could reach. Within minutes, she'd enlisted her dancing friends to scratch her back and other difficult places. Their night of fun was officially over.

"Thanks, Millie," I said. I was touched by her gesture, mischievous though it was.

Millie winked. "Now I'm going to find Begonia."

I turned to Sophie. "Let's call it a night, shall we?"

CHAPTER 18

I sat in front of the impressive house of the head of the vampire coven and simply stared. Here I thought the Mayor's Mansion was a sight to behold. Lord Gilder's estate reminded me of pictures I'd seen of English castles. The façade was constructed of grey flagstone and the stained glass windows were arched. There was even a turret on the right-hand side of the house. I wondered which room was up there.

If I couldn't help Daniel, then at least I could help bring Walter's killer to justice. I needed to feel useful to *someone* in the world, even if I couldn't be to the angel I loved.

As I left the car and climbed the intimidating stairs to the front door, I realized that my palms were sweaty. I was actually nervous to speak with Lord Gilder—not because I found him particularly scary—but because Lord Gilder in his home seemed like a different vampire from Lord Gilder at the town council meeting.

Instead of a doorbell, a rope hung beside the door. Although I gave it a firm tug, I heard no sound. I only had to wait a moment before the heavy door was dragged open. A young gentleman with dark hair and darker eyes greeted me. He wore a formal black suit with a crisp white shirt.

"Good day," he said. "I take it you are here to see Lord Gilder. Unfortunately, you don't seem to have an appointment."

"No, I don't. Please tell him that Emma Hart is here to see him. I think he'll be willing to speak to me." Presumptuous, I knew, but I wanted to catch him off guard. Lord Gilder was smart and if he knew I was coming to talk about Walter, then he would have time to create a plausible story. Even now, I had no doubt that he was more than capable of thinking on his feet. Still, it would give me a chance to observe his reaction and gauge any possible involvement.

"Please come in and I shall see if my lord and master is available."

His lord and master? So it wasn't just his suit that was fancy.

I sat in the foyer and waited, admiring the intricate tapestries on the walls. The interior was more like a medieval castle than a home in the middle of Spellbound. There was no way he created this place without magic.

Lord Gilder appeared in the foyer moments later, looking pleased to see me. "Miss Hart, what a lovely surprise. To what do I owe this honor?"

"Your home is amazing," I said. "I don't think I've ever been in a house this magnificent."

He bowed slightly. "And you've been in Markos's new office, so I'm even more humbled."

"I've been to his headquarters, which is amazing, but it certainly doesn't compare to this." I glanced upward. "I love the turret. Which room is that?"

He suppressed a smile. "Why don't you follow me and I'll show you?"

A house tour? I could barely contain my excitement.

"If you're sure it's not too much trouble," I said. "I don't want to bother you."

"Don't be absurd," he said. "Do you know how few visitors I get? Unless I'm hosting an event, everyone avoids my house like the plague. I think they find it too intimidating. Isn't that right, Bentley?

The butler appeared behind us. "Too right, master. Can I offer the lady a drink?"

I waved him off. "No, thank you."

"Please have two blood orange mimosas ready when we return," Lord Gilder said with a regal air.

Bentley inclined his head. "As you wish, master."

I followed Lord Gilder up the many steps until we reached the steep spiral staircase that led to the turret. My thighs were feeling the burn.

"This must be good exercise for you," I said.

He gave me a vague smile over his shoulder. "To be perfectly honest, I don't come up here very often anymore. I've grown complacent in my old age."

I nearly laughed. Despite his extended life, Lord Gilder didn't look a day over forty-five.

We reached the top and I immediately noticed there was no door. Rather, we stepped straight from the staircase into the room where the curved walls were lined with books.

"It's a library," I breathed.

"I thought you might appreciate it," Lord Gilder said.

I couldn't tear my eyes away from the sheer volume of books. I moved to the nearest wall and began scanning the titles. *Vampire Wishes. Under the Transylvania Moon. Fang Me, Vampire.* I glanced at Lord Gilder in surprise.

"These are romances."

"You seem surprised."

"You don't strike me as the type of man who would enjoy romantic stories." I cringed inwardly. Why would I insult him like that? I didn't know Lord Gilder well enough to make such a sweeping statement.

Thankfully, he found humor in my assessment. "I assure you, not all the books in here are romances, but a healthy portion of them are. I, for one, get swept away by a good love story."

I continued reading the titles on the shelves. Most of them I'd never heard of. "Is there a whole vampire literary scene that I don't know about?"

Lord Gilder smiled, revealing his impressive fangs. "I imagine there is an entire world of literature that you know nothing about. I mean no offense."

"It's too bad you moved away from Dr. Hall. I bet she'd be in your library every day."

Lord Gilder's brow lifted. "Catherine?" He shook his head. "She never struck me as the kind of woman who would enjoy a good romance."

I cast a sidelong glance at him. "I can assure you that she would." I knew it was dangerous to wade into match-making waters with a nut like Catherine Hall, but her love for Lord Gilder was so obvious that I hated to miss the opportunity.

"You used to live next door to her, didn't you?"

Lord Gilder rubbed his chin thoughtfully. "Yes, of course. That was such a long time ago."

"She speaks very highly of you," I said. "Trust me, I haven't known her very long, but she doesn't speak highly of too many people."

This time Lord Gilder tilted his head back and laughed. "So you really have gotten to know her."

"Sounds like she's had an interesting life," I said.

"We all have," Lord Gilder said. "Including you." He clasped his hands behind his back and paced the length of the floor. "Although I expect you are not here to speak to me about Catherine Hall. My instincts tell me that you're here to speak about Walter Rivers."

One step ahead of me. No surprise there. "As a matter fact, I am. How did you know?"

"I heard about his death," Lord Gilder explained. "I also heard that you and Astrid had been to see Quinty. Quinty's office would lead you to Pansy."

"And Pansy would lead to you," I finished for him.

He nodded. "I understand why Pansy would come to you and not the sheriff under the circumstances. She must be devastated. They were so close."

So he knew about the affair too, but chose to keep it quiet.

"Tell me about this invention that Walter was making for you. A flying machine?"

Lord Gilder nodded. "I liked the idea. We're bound to this town for eternity. I envy those of you who can take to the air. Walter thought he could create a safe way for non-magic users to do so as well."

"What went wrong?" I asked.

Lord Gilder paused. "Wrong?"

"Pansy said you and Walter had a disagreement and you withdrew the rest of the funding."

He rubbed his chin. "Ah, I see. Walter didn't tell her the whole truth of the matter. I suppose it's not unexpected."

"You didn't have a disagreement?"

"Oh, we did, but not over the invention. I was quite happy with his progress."

"Then why did you pull the funding?"

He inhaled slowly. "I told you I'm a bit of a romantic. It bothered me to see Walter misapply his sense of propriety."

"What do you mean?"

"Walter and Pansy...They were true love. Anyone who saw them together could feel the spark. It saddened me to think of him wasting his life as well as his wife's. She deserved the chance to find what he'd found with Pansy."

"So you bribed him?"

He shrugged. "Perhaps? Under the terms of our agreement, he was required to tell his wife within ninety days or I would pull the funding." He hesitated. "I don't think he believed I'd go through with it."

"Are you friendly with Marianne?" It seemed odd to be so invested in a relative stranger's happiness.

"It was more about the ideal than the specific person," he explained. "Walter didn't love her. He should have had the courage to let her go. I tried to motivate him, but, alas, I failed."

Lord Gilder had no reason to murder Walter. While he may have meddled in Walter's affairs, he had no personal stake in the matter—no vampire pun intended.

"Speaking of the courage to let someone go, will I be seeing you on Saturday?"

His unexpected question rattled me. "Um, yes. Of course. It's Daniel's special day. I wouldn't miss it for the world."

He gave me a sympathetic smile. "You will find the courage that Walter lacked, of that I have no doubt."

"You're forgetting a crucial distinction, Lord Gilder," I said sadly. "Walter had a choice, whereas I don't. I gave it my best, but the situation is beyond my control now. It isn't courage that dictates my actions. It's acquiescence."

He snorted. "Such big words from such a young mouth. You'd be surprised to learn what you are capable of when your feet are held to the fire," he said.

I stared at a wall of books, pondering his statement. I had no idea what I was capable of when my feet were held to the fire—I only knew that I didn't want to get burned.

CHAPTER 19

NATURALLY SATURDAY WAS another perfect day in Spellbound. Secretly I hoped today would be the day for clouds and the threat of rain, but I knew that wouldn't happen. Not to Elsa. She demanded perfection, even from Mother Nature. From her golden blond hair to her toned body, she didn't have a care in the world. And that was what made the whole Daniel ordeal so infuriating. Elsa Knightsbridge had every advantage in life. A devoted mother. Plenty of money. Beauty and brains to match. She even had a loving fiancé in Jasper before she decided to ditch him for Daniel. She didn't need to do this, but it must've irked her to no end that Daniel had rejected her. This was never about her deep, abiding love for him. It was always about revenge, getting her clutches on the one thing she was denied. At her very core, Elsa was still a spoiled brat.

"I expected you to wear something more provocative," Gareth said, inspecting my tasteful plum-colored dress.

"Provocative? Like the dress from the bachelorette party?" I tried to imagine Daniel's reaction if I showed up at his wedding wearing *that*.

"That wasn't a dress," Gareth said. "It was a tissue."

"Frankly, I'm still shocked I'm planning to attend." I didn't know what I expected to happen. Maybe a plague of frogs raining down from the sky. My plan had failed, so now I was doomed to watch Daniel joined in unholy matrimony to a lying, scheming fairy. She'd given herself quite the daily task —poisoning him with Obsession potion for the rest of her life.

"I'm a wee bit disappointed that I'm going to miss the spectacle," Gareth said. "There's no way this is going off without a hitch."

"I don't know why you would say that," I said. "Elsa always gets her way. If she wants the perfect wedding to the perfect angel, that's exactly what she gets."

Gareth frowned. "Someone is feeling a bit sorry for herself today."

I glared at him. "Can you blame me? I know the truth and yet there's nothing I can do about it. Mayor Knightsbridge destroyed the evidence. Elsa knows I'm on to her. No one will believe me because everyone knows how I feel about Daniel."

"You're tight with the sheriff," Gareth said. "Perhaps Astrid could pull together enough evidence for an arrest."

"That's the problem," I said. "There is no evidence. There's my word against hers. Everyone in town will think it's sour grapes. Like the mayor said, Elsa is beautiful and they cared for each other once. Why not now?"

Gareth fell silent, knowing that I made a good point.

Would it help if I pooped on her head? Sedgwick asked.

I looked over my shoulder to where my familiar sat on his perch. "The petty part of me says please do, but everyone will know you did it for me."

It's the thought that counts, Sedgwick said.

I felt something rough scrape along my calf and glanced

down to see Magpie peering up at me. Even the hell beast felt sorry for me today. Now I really felt down in the dumps.

"I appreciate your support, Magpie," I said. "I know we don't always see eye to eye, mainly because you only have one to spare, but it means a lot to me that you care."

Magpie hissed and swiped at me before scampering out the door.

"That was a supportive gesture in case you were wondering," Gareth said.

"I'll take your word for it," I replied. I checked myself in the mirror one last time, not that it mattered how I looked. Daniel would only have eyes for his bride today…and for the rest of his life. It was too heavy a thought so I pushed it away. Dr. Hall would have to find room in her schedule for all the extra sessions I'd need to get me through the next few decades.

The wind chimes sounded and my heart skipped a beat. It was time to go.

"I wish I could be there to support you," Gareth said softly. "I'm sorry."

I gave him a sad smile. "I know you'll be here to support me when I get back and that's enough."

He bent down and pressed his forehead against mine. "Do you feel that?" he asked.

"I do," I said. It was a slight pressure, but it was there. "Just don't head-butt me. It might actually hurt."

"Go answer the door before he thinks you've changed your mind," Gareth said.

I took a steadying breath and headed downstairs. I opened the door and was surprised to see Markos on my front porch in his minotaur form.

"I thought I would go au naturel today, if you don't mind," he said.

I smiled brightly. "You have no idea how much you've

cheered me up," I said. I reached across the threshold and wrapped my arms around his expanded chest. His fur was as soft as I remembered.

"You look pretty today," he said. "Well, you look pretty every day, but especially this morning."

"Thank you, Markos," I said. "And you look particularly handsome." He was so tall now that there was no way we'd fit in his sleek sports jalopy. "How exactly are we getting to Swan Lake?"

On cue, a large carriage approached. This one was different from the Cinderella-style carriage Elsa had used for her engagement party. This was an open air carriage, which meant that there was no ceiling for Markos to bump his curved horns on. It also meant that everyone in town could see that Markos and I were attending the wedding together. That was sure to set tongues wagging.

"After you, Miss Hart," he said, gesturing me forward.

The elf footman helped me into the carriage first and Markos settled across from me.

"I suppose Gareth is feeling left out," Markos said.

"At this point, FOMO is a chronic condition for him," I said. "But if his progress continues, he'll be attending social events in no time."

Markos's brow furrowed. "What's FOMO?"

"Fear Of Missing Out."

The carriage streaked across town to the eastern border of Spellbound. In fact, half of Swan Lake was within the town border and half was outside of it. I learned this the hard way when I ran toward the water to escape a runaway Sigmund. Daniel swooped down from the cliff and saved me from a watery death, but, in doing so, he brought me inside the border of the cursed town.

The blue water of the lake glistened in the distance and I

saw a floating platform adorned with white streamers and a ceremonial arch.

"I guess they're going to perform their vows on the floating platform," Markos observed.

"Looks that way," I said.

There were already hundreds of guests gathered on the shore of the lake. I spotted most of the town council members, including Lady Weatherby. The twisted antlers of her headdress were adorned with tiny white flowers. She actually looked quite festive. We alighted from the carriage and joined the other guests on the shoreline. Lucy buzzed over to me, her pink wings in a tizzy.

"There you are," Lucy said. "I was wondering if you'd changed your mind."

"I was wondering whether Mayor Knightsbridge was going to change her mind about allowing me to be here," I said, glancing over Lucy's shoulder to where the mayor was greeting guests. Her large blue wings were lined with crystals in honor of the special day.

"You know the mayor," Lucy whispered. "She would never risk the scene on her daughter's big day. Banning you would draw attention away from the bride."

Markos wrapped a large arm around me and squeezed. "No matter what happens today, it's going to be okay."

"We're here," Begonia said, pushing through the throng of bodies. "You won't go through this alone."

"This is my first wedding," Laurel said. "Because I'm the youngest, I always end up getting cut from the guest list."

Sophie patted Laurel on the head. "Don't measure all weddings by this one. I have the sense it will be loud and proud."

I leaned over and whispered to Laurel, "Don't worry. This is my first wedding, too."

"I think everyone in Spellbound is here," Millie said. "Except maybe the Grey sisters."

"Not everyone is invited to the reception, though," I said. I'd have to endure that spectacle without my friends.

"I didn't think you'd want to witness this farce," a voice said.

I turned to see Jasper, Elsa's spurned fiancé. "I could say the same to you."

Jasper smiled grimly. "I wanted to see it happen for myself. Otherwise, I would never believe it was real."

I could wholly relate to that. "Some might say you dodged a bullet."

His brow creased. "I guess that's a human world expression." He shielded his eyes from the sun and scanned the area. "I haven't seen the bride or groom yet. Knowing Elsa, she has some grand entrance planned."

"That sounds about right," I said.

At that moment, a group of white doves flew into the air together and formed the shape of a heart above our heads. The crowd oohed and aahed. Then the birds exploded in a display of white flowers. The petals drifted to the ground, scattering beneath our feet. The blow of a trumpet alerted us to the groom's arrival. Daniel arrived on a magic carpet, which struck me as silly given his beautiful set of wings. Elsa's idea, most likely. The magic carpet landed directly on the floating platform and Daniel rose to his feet with a catlike grace. He looked elegant in his white suit, his ivory wings spread wide and proud behind him. I stared at him, overwhelmed with emotion. I'd often heard the phrase that someone 'is a vision,' but I never truly understood it until this moment.

A lump formed in my throat and I struggled to breathe. Daniel was getting married. To someone else. I couldn't believe this moment was actually happening.

He gazed at the crowd, appearing pleased with the turnout. The spell was likely strong at this hour. I imagined Elsa gave him an extra dose today, to be on the safe side.

A trumpet sounded again, signaling the arrival of the bride. I heard the appreciative noises before I glimpsed her. I followed the crowd's gaze skyward where Elsa flew on the back of a winged white horse. A freakin' Pegasus.

"Spell's bells," Begonia whispered.

Spell's bells, indeed. Where on earth did she find a Pegasus? The magnificent beast glided onto the shore and splashed through the shallow waters, depositing Elsa with her groom on the floating platform.

"Mayor Knightsbridge spared no expense," I heard a voice say behind me.

The Pegasus flew away, leaving me with a clear view of the bride and groom. Elsa looked as beautiful as one would expect. Her golden hair was pulled up in a soft bun with loose tendrils caressing her angular cheekbones. She was a stunning bride. Even I couldn't argue with that.

"Who's performing the ceremony?" I asked. Although I'd never actually been to a wedding, I knew that nonreligious ceremonies sometimes involved a justice of the peace. It seemed odd to me, though, that the mother of the bride would officiate the ceremony. Then again, I didn't put anything past Mayor Knightsbridge. She'd shown herself to be a cold and calculating fairy, same as her daughter.

"There is no officiant," Markos said. "I've seen them a few times during a wedding ceremony, but most residents of Spellbound choose to officiate themselves. It's more of a declaration of love than a formal ceremony."

Looking around, it was hard to see this as anything *but* a formal ceremony. The crowd hushed as Elsa's voice was carried by the breeze.

"Daniel and I thank everyone for coming today to witness

our declarations of love. Today we begin a new chapter in our lives, one that has been written in the stars from the very beginning. No two beings were ever more of a match than we are, as I'm sure anyone who has ever seen us together can attest."

I bristled at her words. *No*, I wanted to scream. *You were not written in the stars. You were written in crayon on a Denny's menu.*

"She seems to have the stars confused with magical drugs," Begonia whispered.

"No kidding," I said quietly.

"If it's any consolation," Markos said, "I don't think anyone here believes a word she says."

"If no one believes her, then why doesn't someone stop the wedding?" I asked.

Markos shrugged. "Daniel is a grown angel. He's also somewhat unpopular here, depending on the demographic. Either way, without hard evidence, I don't think anyone really knows what to do."

I returned my attention to the ceremony where Elsa was still reciting her vows. "It has been said that if at first you don't succeed, try, try again. Today marks the day our efforts have paid off."

"There is no try, only do," I mumbled.

"Who said that? Shakespeare?" Markos asked.

"Yoda," I replied.

"I declare my love for you, Daniel Starr. I declare it in front of all those assembled in Spellbound. May our union be blessed with the fruits of our love and may we be bound together by our everlasting affection for each other."

I wanted to hurl. The sentiment would have been beautiful—if he actually loved her.

Daniel cleared his throat. Apparently it was his turn to

speak. My pulse raced. He clasped her hands in his and gazed into her eyes. I fought another urge to vomit.

"Elsa Mae Knightsbridge. I wronged you many years ago and for that I am eternally sorry. You didn't deserve such treatment and I only hope to make it up to you now every day for the rest of our lives."

My chest ached. The rest of their lives. Daniel was an angel. He was immortal. The idea sickened me. He was imprisoning himself and he didn't even know it. I gazed out at the lake, my jaw tightening when I saw the wooden pier on the other side of the water. An image flashed in my mind of me running the length of it, my feet pounding on the wooden boards until I reached the edge. My car had been barreling down behind me, threatening to crush me to death. The only alternative had been to jump, even though I couldn't swim and my mother had drowned. Still, I had jumped and Daniel had saved me. I'd never believed in angels until that moment. I'd never believed in any type of paranormal creature, not ghosts or vampires or witches. That single moment changed my life forever. Instinctively, I twisted my neck to find the spot on the clifftop where I'd first spotted Daniel from my car. He'd been perched there, ready to jump. If seeing him there wasn't fate, then I didn't know the meaning of the word. Elsa could talk about the alignment of the stars all she liked, but I knew in my heart that Daniel and I were meant for each other. I'd never believed in fate before, but I'd warmed to the idea slowly over time. What were the odds that a human girl from Lemon Grove, Pennsylvania would turn out to be a paranormal trapped by the curse? There was no other explanation. Too many coincidences. It was fate, pure and simple.

Daniel's words rang out, clear and strong, and I immediately recognized the quote from one of the Winnie the Pooh books I'd given to him from the library.

My heart swelled. Somewhere in there was my Daniel, struggling to get out. There was no way Elsa would have written Winnie the Pooh quotes for him to recite. This part was all angel.

Sure enough, Elsa frowned as he spoke, her dissatisfaction with his choice of vows evident.

Daniel continued on to the closing remarks and I held my breath. "And with this ring, I bind us..."

No, don't bind yourself to her, Daniel, I pleaded, knowing no one could hear me. *You're still in there. Break the hold she has on you. Break the spell!*

As he slipped the ring onto her finger, something snapped inside me. I felt the power rise up like a wave riding into shore. Between the power and the momentum, I had no hope of stopping it. The magic ripped through me. When I raised my hand to protect myself, the power shot from my fingertips. Guests screamed as yellow light streamed from me. I watched in horror as the line went straight to Daniel, zapping him unconscious.

He slumped to the floor of the floating platform and I saw the flash of rage across Elsa's beautiful features.

"Daniel," she shrieked. Her wreath was caught by the breeze and drifted into the water, floating away from the bride and groom.

"Oh no," I cried. What had I done?

CHAPTER 20

I FELT a firm hand on my shoulder. "What did you do?" Lady Weatherby's stern voice shocked me to attention. Her expression was both grim and fearful at the same time.

"I don't know," I stammered. "I just said I wanted to break her hold on him."

Everyone watched as Elsa helped Daniel to his feet. He blinked at her.

"What's going on?" he asked groggily.

"Someone tried to use witchcraft on you," Elsa said hotly. "Someone who wanted to ruin our wedding."

Daniel shook his head, clearly confused. "Wedding? What wedding?"

The crowd gasped as Elsa tried to remain calm.

"Our wedding, Daniel," she said in a soothing tone. "Darling, we're getting married this very moment."

Daniel recoiled slightly. "Married? How?" He glanced wildly at the guests gathered on the shoreline and his gaze fell upon me. "Emma? I don't understand."

I sighed with relief. The obsession was over.

"Daniel," I cried. As I moved to rush toward him, the firm

grip of Lady Weatherby held me back and I struggled against her. "Let me go."

"Hush, Miss Hart," she hissed.

"What have you done?" Elsa shrieked at me. "What kind of magic was that?" She glanced helplessly at the assembled guests. "She didn't use a wand. That wasn't any witch magic I've ever seen."

Mayor Knightsbridge fluttered toward me, her features twisted in anger. "What are you?"

"She's a witch," Begonia said, stepping forward. "You know this. The coven tested her when she first came to Spellbound."

Lady Weatherby released her hold on me. "I'm afraid the test is not entirely foolproof."

"Not entirely foolproof?" Mayor Knightsbridge glared at the head of the coven. "In what way?"

Lady Weatherby hesitated. "The potion does not distinguish between close relatives of witches."

Uh oh.

"She's a sorceress," someone yelled.

"Or an enchantress," another voice cried.

I felt the crowd's energy shift. The fear was palpable as guests began to edge away from me.

"Call the sheriff," someone yelled.

"Lock her up," another voice called. This statement was followed by cheers.

I looked around wildly, trying to find a friendly face in the sea of frowns. My heart hammered in my chest and I felt my anxiety skyrocket.

"Please," I said. "It's me. Emma."

The sound of my voice was drowned out by shouts of 'lock her up.' My chest tightened and I began to run, pushing my way through the crowd. I needed to get away.

"Stop her," someone screamed. Elsa.

As I cleared the mass of bodies, I felt strong arms around my waist. Suddenly my feet were off the ground and I was airborne.

"I've got you," Daniel said. "Just don't wiggle too much or I might drop you. Something we'd both regret."

I squeezed my eyes closed as we rose above the cliffside. I'd already been fighting to keep down breakfast throughout the ceremony and being hundreds of feet in the air wasn't helping.

"Don't worry. No one's coming after us," Daniel said.

I couldn't answer. I was in too much shock.

"Where are we going?" I finally managed to ask. I surveyed the area and realized we were near the cave of the Grey sisters.

"Somewhere safe."

"You think I need to be kept safe?" I asked softly. "From the residents of Spellbound?" From my friends?

"The pitchforks are out," Daniel said. "You don't want to be near them until they calm down. Distance is the best answer."

Although my feet scraped the ground, my legs crumpled and I fell in a heap. Daniel slid a hand underneath my armpit and lifted me to my feet.

"You're shaking," he said quietly.

"Can you blame me?" I tried to quell the wave of nausea that continued to plague me.

He wrapped his arms around me, holding me close, and I felt the tickle of his white wings. "I'm sorry."

"You have nothing to be sorry for," I said. "It's not your fault."

"I don't know exactly what happened, but I get the sense that if it weren't for me, you wouldn't have used your sorceress magic."

And I'd do it again, knowing it would save him.

There you are. I've been searching everywhere for you.

I glanced skyward to see Sedgwick circling above us.

"Sedgwick, what are you doing here?"

Making sure you're not dead.

"Still alive, thank you very much."

You caused quite the uproar. Well done.

"I'm glad you approve."

So what's next? It's not like you can leave town.

I glanced at Daniel. "What's next?"

"I think we should hide out with the Grey sisters until things calm down. They like you. They'll protect you if anyone comes knocking."

"Will you let Gareth know?" I called to Sedgwick.

I'll do my best to communicate with him, but, fair warning, I don't speak lower level species.

"Do your best."

Stay safe, he replied and flew off.

Daniel rubbed the spot between my shoulder blades. "Ready?"

I nodded and we made our way to the mouth of the cave.

"The heart of darkness has entered the cave, she has," the shorter Grey sister said.

"Hey, who are you calling the heart of darkness?" I objected. "I bought your sister teeth and a new pair of eyes."

"A fair trade," the taller sister said.

"So we have a favor to ask," Daniel said.

"A favor?" the shorter one queried. "From the Grey sisters?"

"Yes, you," Daniel replied. "Emma and I need a place to hide out for a bit. We figured this is one of the last places anyone would want to...I mean, would think to look."

"You are most welcome here, you are," Lyra said. "Your secret has been discovered, I take it."

Tears stung my eyes. "It has."

"And they have turned on you, they have," the shorter one said.

"No surprise to us," the taller one chimed in. "The curse serves as no reminder."

"Too far gone. They have all forgotten," Lyra said.

"You think the curse was to punish them all?" I asked. "I thought it was because of…" I halted and cast a furtive glance at Daniel.

"I told you my story," he said matter-of-factly. "I can't say for certain the curse wasn't because of me, but I don't think it was."

"Some of the residents weren't even born when the curse took hold," I said. "It isn't fair to the innocent ones."

"And what have they learned, my pet?" Lyra asked. "Did anyone speak up for you?"

"Some tried," I said, thinking of Begonia's effort. "And Daniel…"

Lyra clucked her tongue. "They learn nothing, they do."

We made our way further into the cave and I tried to ignore the gloomy and depressing interior. I was lucky to be here—criticizing the lack of decor and modern amenities was ungrateful, to say the least.

The sisters circled Daniel. "You act upon your own free will, you do," Lyra said.

"I do, thanks to Emma," he replied.

"I don't know what I did," I admitted. "Some kind of sorcery."

"My mind is beginning to clear," Daniel said. "When I first snapped out of it, I felt confused."

"You didn't seem to know where you were," I said. "Do you remember everything now?"

He rubbed his chin, thinking. "I remember, but it feels like an out-of-body experience. Like it happened to someone else and I watched it."

Panic crept through my veins. "Do you remember anything aside from Elsa?" *Like my confession of love at the Spellbound Care Home?*

He laughed. "I remember the bachelor party if that's what you're about. You created quite the mess there."

"Because I was trying to test all of the Anti-Obsession potions on you!"

He grinned. "And you did a bang-up job."

I elbowed him in the ribs. "Hey. I was trying to rescue you. Next time I'll let you get married."

"We're sorry we came without gifts," Daniel said. "We don't mean to offend you."

"None taken," Petra said. "Circumstances are unusual, they are."

"We hope we haven't put you in any danger," I said.

The Grey sisters gave a collective scoff.

"Impossible, that is," Effie said. "The Grey sisters are both feared and revered."

I didn't argue with that.

"Come and find comfort in our home," Lyra said, gesturing for us to enter an offshoot of the main cave.

Comfort was a stretch. The room was as Spartan as the main cave area. Other than a few fey lanterns and chairs, there wasn't much to look at. I really hoped we didn't need to hide here for very long.

"Now you will be able to practice your magic openly," Lyra said, a gleam in her two eyes.

"I can't practice what I don't know," I replied.

"Learn you must," Petra said. "Control the magic before it controls you."

Daniel removed his suit jacket and tie. "This is suffocating."

"And absurdly unattractive," Lyra said. "Burn it for you, I will."

A slow grin stretched his lips. "Actually, I'd like to do the honors, if you don't mind."

"This way to the fire," the middle Grey sister said, crooking a thin finger.

"Are you sure?" I asked. "It's a really nice jacket." Ricardo would be bawling his wereferret eyes out if he knew.

"I'd burn the whole suit right now if I had something else to wear," Daniel said.

"Overrated, clothing is," Lyra said with a crude smile.

I shot her a quizzical look before turning to Daniel. "Start with the jacket and tie. The rest can go later."

We followed Lyra back to the main area of the cave where a fire burned low. I noticed holes in the stone above for ventilation.

Daniel tossed the jacket and tie into the flames and together we watched them burn.

"I'm sorry for what she did to you," I said.

"Why are you sorry, Emma? You're not responsible for her actions." He continued to stare at the flames as they licked the remnants of fabric.

"I just wish I could have done more to help you, so that things didn't go as far as they did. I made so many attempts to...to make things right." Emotions bubbled up in my throat. All of the feelings I'd been repressing began pushing their way to the surface.

"I know you did," he said softly. "And I would have done the same for you."

Despite the massive size, the cave was beginning to feel claustrophobic. As if sensing my distress, Daniel extended his hand. "Why don't we go for a walk? Fresh air might do us both some good."

"Bring back a rabbit, you will," Lyra said from beside the crackling fire.

I cast a sidelong glance at Daniel. "That one's all you."

. . .

We walked in companionable silence until I recognized the path to Curse Cliff.

"We should probably turn back before it gets dark," I said. Although I didn't share the fear that some residents had about the cliff, I didn't love the idea of wandering around out here in the pitch black.

"In a minute," Daniel said. "There's something I need to say first."

"Okay." I slowed my walk.

"I lied to you," he said.

My feet ground to a halt. I wasn't sure I heard him correctly. "Lied to me? What do you mean?"

He inhaled deeply and focused on me. "When you asked me what else I remembered, I pretended that you meant the bachelor party."

I blinked in confusion. "Why? Are you embarrassed about your time with Elsa? Because you don't need to be. Everyone knows it was a magic potion."

"I'm not talking about Elsa. Ever again." He took my hand. "I meant my time with you. At the Spellbound Care Home."

Oh no. He remembered.

My heart thundered in my chest. "You mean when I told you..." Spell's bells. When I told him...

"That you loved me."

My throat became dry and I couldn't swallow. "Did I?"

His features softened. "You did."

"Maybe it was the potion..."

He shook his head slowly. "Not a potion."

My body was on fire. I couldn't tell whether it was from desire or embarrassment or both.

"Daniel, I..."

Before I could finish, he lowered his lips to mine and

kissed me. It started softly and slowly and my hands drifted to his back where his wings were tucked behind him. The feathers felt like silk beneath my fingertips. As the kiss intensified, a gentle moan escaped my lips and he pulled me closer. When we finally broke apart for air, I noticed that he was grinning.

"What's so funny?" I demanded.

"I'm not smiling because anything's funny," he said. "I'm smiling because I'm happy."

My legs were ready to slide out from under me. "Are you sure I haven't done some wacky sorcery and transferred your obsession to me?"

He wrapped his arms around me. "I love you, Emma Hart. There's no wacky sorcery. No potion. Only you."

I couldn't quite believe my ears. "You love me?"

"Of course I love you."

"Why?" My love for him made sense. He was...Daniel. A perfect angelic specimen.

He gripped me by the shoulders and gazed into my eyes. "I'll tell you why. You're the sweetest, most compassionate, bravest person I've ever known, and I've known a lot of people. You make me laugh. You humble me. I'm a better version of myself with you than I ever was without you."

I tried to process the words. I wasn't very adept at accepting compliments. "What about pretty?" I finally asked. "You didn't say I was pretty."

He howled with laughter. "I didn't think superficial compliments were your thing. Yes, Emma. I think you're very pretty."

I smiled and hugged him. "I didn't know it was possible to feel this happy."

Daniel sighed and stroked my hair. "Me neither."

Unfortunately, our moment of happiness was short-lived. I heard a dull roar in the distance. At first I mistook the sound for an incoming thunderstorm until I remembered that this was Spellbound.

"What is that?" I asked.

Beside me, Daniel straightened. "I hear hoofbeats." He paused to listen. "And feet. Many feet. I think our location has been discovered."

Uh oh. An angry mob was headed our way and we had nowhere to run.

Daniel placed a protective arm around my waist. "We can fly somewhere else. Just say the word."

I drew a deep breath. "Let's give them a chance. Maybe they've come to apologize."

CHAPTER 21

THEY DIDN'T COME to apologize.

I sensed their anger and frustration as they approached, a giant, fast-moving cloud of frowns and fists.

"There she is," a voice shouted.

A wave of nausea slammed into me as they moved closer, shouting and gesticulating angrily. All of this over magic I didn't even understand.

I clasped Daniel's hand in mine and he glanced down at me, a question in his turquoise eyes. They asked me if I wanted to flee. I wasn't sure.

The crowd pressed toward us, and Daniel and I backed slowly onto Curse Cliff. I glanced behind me to see the steep drop below. Were they really going to run me off the side and into oblivion like the wicked stepmother in Disney's *Snow White*? For some reason, Daniel's wings were a small consolation. It was the betrayal that hurt the most. These residents had become my friends. My family. But now I was a known sorceress and they looked at me with only fear in their eyes.

Fear.

My heart thawed a little. I understood fear—empathized with it, even when misdirected at me.

"Grab them," a woman's voice cried out. Myra, the church administrator, pushed her way to the front of the group. "We can't let them get away."

"Get away?" I queried. "We're all trapped here. Where do you think we're going to go, except to plunge to our deaths?"

"He won't," Myra said, jerking a thumb toward Daniel. "It's whether he's with us or against us. If he flies off and carries you with him, then he's against us."

"This is ridiculous." Laurel appeared next to Myra. "Many of us know Emma. She's not evil. Far from it. She's done nothing but help people since she got here."

"Maybe that's part of her master plan," Myra said. "Lull us into a false sense of security."

"She didn't know she was a witch...or a sorceress before she came," Begonia objected, joining Laurel at the front of the crowd.

"But when she found out she was a sorceress, she didn't tell anyone." Hugo said. "If that doesn't smack of guilt, then I don't know what does."

Daniel stepped in front of me, putting himself between the angry mob and me.

"It was my idea to keep it secret," he admitted. "Because this was exactly what I feared would happen."

"Hand her over," a voice shouted.

"So you can do what?" Daniel replied. "Throw her in Swan Lake and see if she floats? We already know what she is. More importantly, we already know *who* she is."

"Do we?" Myra asked. "Or has it been an act? I always thought her sweet nature was suspicious. Nobody is that nice."

"Maybe in your mirror that's true," Begonia snapped.

"Emma is genuine. She has been from the moment she stepped inside Spellbound."

"She wants the criminals to run free," Hugo said, loudly enough for everyone to hear. "She's been begging for this committee to revise the sentencing guidelines so that she can make sure proven criminals get off without serving their time."

"That's not true," I said. "Sentencing in Spellbound is draconian. It..."

"Dracula had nothing to do with drafting laws here," someone interjected.

I resisted the urge to smack my forehead.

The shape of an enormous minotaur moving through the crowd caught everyone's attention, including mine. Markos moved to the front to address the mob.

"I cannot believe we are standing on Curse Cliff, trying to persecute one of our own." His deep voice reverberated across the desolate landscape. Even the ground seemed to shake beneath my feet.

"She's not one of our own," Myra cried. "That's the point. She'll kill us all before we ever have a chance to break the curse."

"The fact that she's standing on Curse Cliff speaks volumes." Fabio, the werelion, stepped forward. "That ground is as evil as the woman who created the curse."

Daniel turned back to me. "Your date with him really did not go well, did it?"

I shrugged.

I recognized the twisted antlers of Lady Weatherby's headdress as she maneuvered through the crowd. Residents moved aside to make a path for her. Her stony features gave nothing away.

She raised her wand in the air and signaled for the mob's attention. "Residents of Spellbound. Hear me now."

The crowd fell silent. When I realized I was holding my breath, I gently exhaled.

"I assume I need no introduction. As the head of the coven that agreed to take custody of Miss Hart, I take full responsibility for her presence here. The spell we used to determine her true nature would not have made a distinction between witch, sorceress, and enchantress. As you already know, these three are closely aligned. It would be like trying to identify whether someone is of Norwegian ancestry versus that of a Swede using only DNA."

"What's a Swede?" someone called.

"I think it's a type of potato," someone else replied.

"No one blames you, Lady Weatherby," Hugo said, ever the butt kisser.

"I'm not asking for absolution," she said coolly and I bit back a smile. Take that grumpy centaur.

"What's your solution?" Myra asked. "What do we do with her?"

"I do not understand the need to *do* anything," Lady Weatherby replied. "My witches are correct. Miss Hart has proven herself time and time again to be a productive member of our community. Am I pleased with this turn of events? No, I am most certainly not. But a sorceress with unchecked and unmastered power is far more dangerous. I propose that we continue as before. The coven accepts responsibility for the continued training of Miss Hart."

A gasp rippled through the crowd.

"Train her?" Fabio repeated. "So that she can curse us worse than the enchantress one day?"

"Continue to treat her with such hostility and maybe she will," Lady Weatherby said. "And maybe I will approve of her actions."

Mike, the wereweasel I spent an unlucky evening with at Shamrock Casino, raised his hand. "What makes you think you can control her? What if she grows more powerful than even you?"

Lady Weatherby turned to give me an appraising look. "If she does, then perhaps she can break the curse that has long kept us prisoner here. Why do we not look past the fear and see the value in her potential power?"

Her mention of breaking the curse got their attention.

"Break the curse?" someone echoed. "Do you think she can?"

Lady Weatherby lowered her head slightly. "That I cannot say for certain, but the coven has made efforts for years to no avail. Perhaps a sorceress would be better equipped."

Me? Break the curse? I couldn't even do a simple defensive spell without screwing it up. That seemed like an awfully bold statement.

"Lady Weatherby," I dared to say. "I don't think…"

"Do not think at all right now, child," she said. "I have the mob's attention. Now is a time to move." She lowered her voice. "To safety, if possible."

Wait a second. Lady Weatherby was…on my side? To say I was stunned was an understatement.

"Where do I take her?" Daniel asked quietly. "Where's safe? We can't go back to the Grey sisters now that we've been discovered."

Nor did I want to. That cave was more depressing than a vampire without fangs.

A thought occurred to me. "I know where we can go that no one will follow."

"Where?" Daniel asked.

"Take me in your arms and I'll show you."

Raisa's cottage was just as eerie as the last time I'd been here. The bone fence and the skull above the door of the small cottage set my teeth on edge. Smoke billowed from the chimney. Once again, Raisa seemed to be expecting me.

"Are you sure about this?" Daniel asked.

"It'll be fine," I said. "She's a ghost. Just don't let her bite you. Her teeth are iron. Nasty little suckers."

"If she's a ghost, then I won't be able to see her."

Good point.

The door creaked open and I ushered Daniel inside. I glanced around the familiar sparse interior for signs of Raisa. She stood in front of the bubbling cauldron in the Inglenook-style fireplace. Her skeletal frame was as unsettling as I remembered. Her legs were like two knitting needles and her skin was covered in brown spots. With her bald patches and stringy grey and white hair, Raisa wasn't going to win any beauty competitions.

"She's a looker, isn't she?" Daniel whispered.

"You can see her?" I asked quietly.

"And I can hear both of you," Raisa said, setting aside the pot stirrer.

"Why can he see you?" I asked. I thought seeing ghosts was my special ability.

"I'm not like your vampire roommate," Raisa said. "My afterlife is…unique. I am tied to the land in a way that your vampire is not."

Well, I guess that explained why I could see Raisa. Everyone could see Raisa. They just didn't know it because residents were too afraid to come to the old bone cottage. Even in death, Raisa was one of the most intimidating members of the Spellbound community.

"So they've thrown you to the wolves," Raisa said, clicking her iron teeth together. "Not surprised. Not surprised at all."

"I am," I said. "I thought…"

She peered at me. "You thought what? That you would be any different? Ah, that's the whole problem. You are different and it terrifies them. The unknown terrifies most creatures."

"I don't think it's that I'm different," I countered. "Spellbound is all about diversity. I think it's because of the town's history. The curse."

"I agree," Daniel said. "There's an unconscious bias."

"No one asked to hear from you, lost angel," Raisa snapped. "You give them too much credit, sorceress. They have turned on you and yet you still give them the benefit of the doubt."

"Because I know them, maybe better than they know themselves." I thought about all of the acts of kindness and support I'd seen since my arrival. The residents of Spellbound weren't bad or malicious. They cared about each other. They cared about me. They were just scared right now. A knee-jerk reaction that hopefully would fade once reason took hold.

"The potion doesn't lie," Raisa said. "You truly are pure of heart, aren't you?"

Daniel snaked an arm around my waist and squeezed. "She really is. I would be lost without her."

Raisa glared at him. "You are lost. She has only found herself."

"We thought maybe we could stay here until everyone calmed down," I said.

She cackled. "Because no one would dare come here in search of you. Is that it?"

Pretty much. "We tried to stay with the Grey sisters…"

Raisa flicked a dismissive bony finger. "The Grey sisters. Those cave dwellers are useless. You'll stay with me until you're ready to return." She gave me a pointed look. "*If* you're ever ready to return."

"I'll be ready," I said. I certainly wasn't making plans to redecorate the bone cottage. Talk about lipstick on a pig.

"Now who's ready for a nice cup of tea?" she asked.

"I would love one," I said. "But no secret potions this time. Promise?"

Raisa cackled. "Where's the fun in that? You need to give an old witch her chance for amusement." Somehow I knew Raisa and I differed on what constituted amusement.

A knock on the door startled everyone, including Raisa.

"Who's that?" I asked, stiffening.

"How should I know?" Raisa said. "I'm staring at the closed door same as you."

"But you know things," I said. "You can see beyond the veil."

Raisa suppressed a smile. "You learn well, pet. Open the door and let us see our surprise guest."

Insistent tapping continued on the door. Finally a familiar voice rang out, "Let me in, you foolish nincompoops. I'm freezing my butt off out here. This gown doesn't close in the back."

Spell's bells. "Agnes?"

I raced to the door and yanked it open. Sure enough, Agnes stood on the doorstep wearing nothing except what appeared to be a black hospital gown that tied in the back. Stars and stones. Was her butt exposed to the elements all the way from the Spellbound Care Home?

"Invite me in," Agnes insisted.

"Get in here," I said. "You're not a vampire." And I knew that wasn't even true for vampires.

Agnes stepped over the threshold and her gaze went straight to Raisa. "Raisa. As I live and breathe. Unlike you."

"Agnes of the coven. We meet again."

I moved to stand between them. "You two be nice. Agnes, how did you get here?"

Agnes flashed me a mischievous smile. "I heard all about the kerfuffle. I waited until my afternoon appointment. Boyd came to give me my monthly exam. The room they use is right by the entrance so I knew it was my best shot of getting out."

"The Spellbound Care Home is all the way across town," I said. "You couldn't possibly have walked all the way here."

Agnes shrugged her bony shoulders. "I may have commandeered a jalopy and left it somewhere near the Oaks to throw people off the trail. I knew you'd come here."

"How?" I asked.

She smiled. "Because that's exactly what I would have done." She glanced at Raisa. "No one in their right mind would come here willingly."

"Would you like a cup of tea, Agnes?" Raisa asked in her most polite tone.

"Tea? Do I look like a harpy to you? Don't you have anything stronger?"

Ah, there was the Agnes I knew.

"Of course. I thought you'd never ask." Raisa went over to the shelf and pulled down a bottle of Rattle Rum. She poured a small glass for Agnes. "Anyone else?"

"Go on, sorceress," Agnes teased. "I think it'll do you good under the circumstances. Loosen up that knot that you mistakenly call a body."

I wasn't sure about this. The last time I dared to drink with Agnes, I found myself cradling the toilet of her care home bathroom. I wasn't keen to repeat the experience in Raisa's bone-infested cottage.

"I'll have one," Daniel said.

My head jerked toward him. "Really?"

"It seems like the thing to do at the moment," he said, with a trace of amusement.

"Peer pressure," I mused. "Okay, fine. Me too."

Raisa clapped her hands together. "Excellent." She poured three more glasses and distributed them.

"Bottoms up," Agnes quipped. "Or out, as the case may be." She shook her exposed butt and I winced.

"Raisa, do we have any clothes for Agnes to wear?"

The two women stared at me.

"It's called magic," Agnes said. "Lend me your wand, nincompoop."

I placed my hands on my hips. "I will if you ask nicely," I said firmly. "Stop calling me names."

"Nincompoop is a term of endearment," Agnes said. "Do you think I call everybody that?"

I relented, pulling out my wand. Knowing Agnes, she was telling the truth.

She snatched the wand and pointed it to herself. "Red as a rose/give me new clothes."

I watched as her black hospital gown stretched into a black tracksuit. All that was missing was the white Adidas logo.

Agnes glanced down at her attire. "Comfy and cool. Nice work for an old witch."

"May I make a toast?" Daniel asked.

"By all means," Agnes said. "Then I get to have another drink." She held out her empty glass for Raisa to refill.

I looked up at Daniel. "A toast to what? Our banishment?"

He raised his glass. "I'd like to make a toast to Emma. For believing in me. For seeing what was in my heart when no one else did. For seeing the good in everyone, even in the face of doubt."

Raisa and Agnes raised their glasses. "To Emma," they said in unison.

"Well, Agnes, I think this might be the first time we have ever agreed on something," Raisa said.

"Don't get used to it," Agnes said.

"Agnes, they'll come looking for you," I said. "People will be worried."

She blew a raspberry. "Worry about me? Are you serious? Trust me, they're more worried about the damage I can do out of the care home than they are about what might happen to me."

I didn't doubt that. Agnes was capable of much mayhem when she set her mind to it. I'd seen it firsthand when she'd stolen my wand and wreaked havoc in the cafeteria. On that note, I retrieved my wand from her grasp.

"You can't keep my wand," I said, tucking it back into my waistband.

"You know you don't need that thing," Agnes said. "You're a sorceress. Your magic is different."

"I know," I said. "But it doesn't mean I can't use the wand. There are still spells I can do that I learned at the academy."

Agnes frowned. "Yes, the academy. They will be struggling to know what to do with you."

"They've already decided what to do with her," Raisa said. "They want her cast out, like me."

"I wouldn't be so sure about that," Daniel said. "Lady Weatherby is the one who bought us time to come here. She's appealing to the citizens to let her continue to train Emma."

Raisa's eyes rounded at the news and I worried that one of them would pop out of the socket like it did the last time I was here. I wasn't in the mood to play catch-the-eyeball.

"Agnes of the coven, did I really just hear that your replacement made a reasonable decision? Times surely have changed." Raisa clucked her tongue.

"Jacinda Ruth may be uptight and rigid, but she is my daughter and I know her well. It doesn't surprise me in the least that she is one of the first to come around."

"Like she was with you?" Daniel challenged her. "I haven't seen her glued to your bedside."

Agnes lowered her head. "We will take time, I recognize this, but it will happen. She's already been to see me since the youth spell. Some relationships require more care than others. You of all people should know that." She gave him a pointed look.

I polished off the rest of the alcohol in my glass and tried to ignore the burn in my throat. I couldn't understand the appeal of the stuff. It was vile.

"How long do you plan to hide out here?" Agnes asked.

Daniel and I exchanged looks. We hadn't gotten that far in the conversation.

"Until Spellbound calms down and Emma is safe," Daniel said. "It only takes one resident to do something stupid."

The idea unnerved me. I'd investigated enough murder cases since my arrival to worry that he was right.

"You are welcome to seek refuge here for as long as it's needed, pet," Raisa said. "You can always put a glamour on the cottage so that no one can see it. Even if they came looking, they wouldn't find you."

"I could do that?" I queried.

"It's a basic spell for a sorceress," Raisa said. "It would be more complicated for a garden variety coven witch."

Agnes nodded. "She speaks the truth. You have untapped, raw power, Emma."

"I don't really want to hide for any length of time," I said, hating the idea of leaving Gareth and Magpie alone for too long. Sedgwick could fend for himself. "I'd only like to give everyone a chance to process the news and be rational."

Raisa snorted. "You may overestimate them then."

I gave my head an adamant shake. "No. I don't think so. They're good-hearted. Every single one of them." Even the ones I didn't particularly like—Jemima, Hugo—I believed they'd come around in the end.

"I want to help you," Agnes said. "Tell me what I can do. I may be old and tucked away in a home, but I can still be of use, whether my coven believes it or not."

"I believe in you, Agnes," I said. And I believed in me, too. "You know what? I'm not going to hide here at all."

Daniel flinched. "What do you mean?"

"I mean I'm going home."

Daniel glared at Raisa. "What did you put in the alcohol?"

I touched his arm lightly. "Nothing, Daniel. I'm not drunk or under a spell. I think going home and facing reality is the best option. I'll put another protective spell around my house if I have to, but I'm not going to let fear control the situation."

"Sometimes fear is healthy..." Daniel began.

I stopped him with a look. "I'm going home, Daniel. If I stay here, it feels like giving up."

Raisa nodded solemnly. "I do not disagree, pet. When I turned my back on Spellbound, it was a form of giving up. I never did work through it."

No. She became complacent and died alone. And I refused to let that be my fate.

CHAPTER 22

WE LANDED on the road in front of my house and I was shocked to discover a crowd already gathered on my front porch. My first instinct was to grip Daniel's shirt, but he gently dislodged my fingers.

"Look closely," he said. "They're carrying flowers, not pitchforks."

Flowers? I squinted. Sure enough, I saw flashes of color between the familiar bodies of my friends.

My friends.

The remedial witches were there, of course, along with Astrid and Britta. The friendly neighborhood harpies. Markos, Demetrius and his crew, the Gorgon sisters, and Lord Gilder. I inhaled softly, drinking in the moment. Alex held a sign that must have been left over from the shifter protest. *Piss Off* was crossed out and replaced with *We Love You, Emma.*

Astrid approached us as we came up the walkway. "You okay?"

I nodded, struggling to get my emotions under control. "What happened after we left Swan Lake?"

"Chaos," Astrid said. "I went straight to Elsa's and unearthed where she'd stashed the Obsession potion. She's in custody now, demanding to wear her wedding dress instead of the regulation jumpsuit."

Naturally. "Is her use of the potion on an unknowing participant considered a major crime?"

I thought about all the times I'd dabbled with magic and made a mess of it, most recently at Daniel's bachelor party. No one was planning to arrest me. On the other hand, Elsa's use of magic was almost like kidnapping or holding someone against his will. When I thought of it that way, it seemed much more serious than magical brownies.

"Abuse of magic tends to be a lesser charge," Astrid said, "but Elsa's abuse is fairly egregious."

I didn't disagree.

"Daniel, when you have time, I'd like to ask you a few questions," Astrid said. "You probably know more than you think you do."

He kissed the top of my head. "I'd like to get this one settled in first, if that's okay."

"I don't think a quiet evening is in the cards for her yet," Astrid said. "I think she'll want to join me for my next stop."

My brow creased. "Where are you going?"

"To the Mayor's Mansion," Astrid replied. "I hope we can resolve this peacefully."

I blinked. "Peacefully? Wait. What?"

"Mayor Knightsbridge is being charged with obstruction of justice and the destruction of crucial evidence in a criminal matter. I'm going over to arrest her now."

I gulped. "You're *arresting* Mayor Knightsbridge?"

Astrid cast me a sidelong glance. "Of course. What did you think would happen?"

I felt torn. On the one hand, I understood why. On the other hand, she was protecting her daughter. If my mother had lived, I had no doubt she would have been similarly devoted to me.

"Will she need to step down as mayor?" I asked.

"If she doesn't step down voluntarily, then she'll be forcibly removed."

I blew out a breath. "All of this because of me."

Astrid's blue eyes bulged. "Because of *you*? Emma Hart, are you out of your mind?"

My shoulders sagged. "If I hadn't insisted on proving Elsa's guilt and stealing the vial, the mayor wouldn't be in this predicament. I'm the one who brought the vial to her."

Astrid grabbed me by the shoulders and stared at me. "Listen to me right now. You are not responsible for this. These women are grown fairies that know better. The mayor is responsible for her actions. Elsa is responsible for her actions. You did not create this mess. Understood?"

I sniffed. "I guess. So will the council elect a new mayor?"

Astrid released her grip on me. "No, we'll hold an election. The council will probably appoint an interim mayor, though."

"Lucy?" I asked hopefully.

"Most likely. She did a commendable job when the mayor was under the youth spell."

A silver lining at last. Lucy deserved the town's trust.

"Astrid, do you think the mayor will come quietly?"

Astrid snorted. "Hell no. That's why I'm not going alone."

"I don't know that I'm going to be enough…"

"Not just you," Astrid said. "I've asked the entire town council to meet me at the mansion."

Oh.

"Peer pressure?" I queried.

"To start with," Astrid said. "Lady Weatherby is prepared to use more forceful methods of persuasion, though."

What a day. I felt for my wand along my waistband. Even

though I technically didn't need it to perform magic, I liked knowing it was there. A security blanket.

Daniel squeezed my hand. "Good luck."

"Ready?" Astrid asked.

"Never, but that doesn't seem to stop me from moving forward."

The members of the town council stood in a semi-circle outside the Mayor's Mansion when we arrived. No one looked pleased by the turn of events. My knee-jerk reaction was to apologize. Years of training by my tough grandmother.

"Why are you sorry?" Lady Weatherby snapped. "You've done nothing wrong here."

"I feel like this is all my fault," I admitted.

"Lying about your origin is your fault," Lorenzo Mancini said coolly. "This matter rests entirely in the lap of Mayor Knightsbridge and her daughter."

"But lying about her origin isn't a crime," Maeve pointed out. "And, as far as I'm concerned, her reasons for withholding this information were justified. It's not like she showed up in Spellbound, knowing what she truly was."

"We'll never know for certain, will we?" Lorenzo asked.

"We do know," I said. "Because I told you that."

Lorenzo glared at me. "The way you told us you were a witch?"

"I never told you I was anything but human," I argued. "You told me I was a witch at the emergency town council meeting. Or have you conveniently forgotten?"

Lorenzo's jaw tightened. At least he stopped talking.

Security guards appeared at the oversized front door, their expressions grim. Not a good sign.

"Step aside, Cameron," Wayne said to the guard on the left. A fellow troll.

"I'm afraid I can't, sir," Cameron replied. "Mayor's orders."

Lady Weatherby swept up the front steps, her black cloak dragging behind her. "And the town council's orders are to step aside."

"We work for the mayor," the other guard said. "We don't answer to the town council, ma'am."

"I'm not ma'am," she hissed. "I am Lady Weatherby, the head of the coven in Spellbound. Now move aside before I turn you both into toads. Permanently."

The two guards exchanged glances before opting to abandon their posts.

Lady Weatherby pushed open the doors and stepped into the grand foyer. The rest of us trailed behind her. Lucy fluttered toward us, her wings twitching anxiously.

"The mayor is indisposed…" Lucy began.

"In the name of the town council, where is she?" Lord Gilder demanded.

Lucy drifted to the floor. "In her office."

The group moved down the hall without another word. Although they weren't quite the angry mob that chased me onto Curse Cliff, this smaller group was far more intimidating.

Lady Weatherby didn't bother to knock. She tapped the door with her wand and it blew off the hinges and onto the office floor. Talk about a badass.

"Mayor Knightsbridge," she said, breezing into the room with her usual air of regal authority. "We are here to remove you from your office."

Juliet held up a finger. "Both literally and figuratively, I might add."

Mayor Knightsbridge remained behind her desk,

clutching her wand. "You don't have the authority. The vote needs to be unanimous and I disagree."

"Your vote doesn't count under the circumstances," Maeve said.

"You're loving this, aren't you?" the mayor spat at her. "You've always been competitive with me."

Maeve frowned. "Believe me when I tell you that this brings me no pleasure whatsoever. You are one of us, but you've broken our trust. You've broken everyone's trust."

"I had to protect my Elsa," the mayor objected. "Can't you understand that?"

"I can and I do," Maeve said gently. "But if Elsa had committed murder and you helped her hide the body and lied to law enforcement about it, you'd be facing charges then, wouldn't you?"

"That's different," the mayor insisted. "We're not talking about a murder. We're talking about a marriage. She's a gorgeous fairy who would have doted on him. Daniel never would have known that he was unhappy with her. And if he doesn't know, how is that harmful?"

"Because it wasn't real," I shouted. It was infuriating. Did she really not understand how wrong it was?

"Who's to say what's real?" the mayor asked. "If Daniel believed their love was real, why does it matter that it was fueled by a potion?"

Lady Weatherby looked down her aquiline nose at the mayor. "If you cannot see the line in the sand, then I cannot help you."

"I see the line," the mayor said. "Only it's in a different place from yours and not so deeply embedded."

"Lay down your wand," Astrid said, stepping forward. "We'd like to do this peacefully and without magic."

Mayor Knightsbridge surveyed the group assembled in front of her that included some of the most powerful figures in Spellbound. By herself, she didn't stand a chance and she knew it.

"Fine," she said, and offered her wand to Lady Weatherby. "I'll go without a fight, but I am telling you now, I will not spend a single night in a prison cell."

Astrid placed a clamp on the mayor's blue wings to keep her from flying away. "I'm afraid that won't be up to you."

"Mayor Knightsbridge, we hereby relieve you of your duties as mayor of Spellbound," Lord Gilder said.

"We appoint Lucy Langtree as interim mayor," Juliet added.

Lucy fluttered into the office, her face ashen. She'd clearly been eavesdropping outside the doorway. "Are you sure?"

"We can think of no better replacement until the election can be held," Lorenzo said.

Lucy broke into a bright smile. "Oh my goodness. Thank you. I promise to do my best to serve this town."

"We know you will, Lucy," Wayne said.

Astrid escorted the disgraced mayor from the mansion on foot. No fluttering for the fairy. "Now you and Elsa can be roommates again. If you're lucky, maybe she'll let you have the lower bunk."

The mayor scowled as she passed by me. "This is your fault, Emma Hart. Don't think for one second I will ever forget it."

My stomach churned. A mortal enemy. That was all I needed in Spellbound.

I felt a supportive hand on my shoulder. "Pay her no heed," Lord Gilder said. "She'll be stripped of her powers at the very least."

"They'll take away her wand, even if she doesn't serve prison time?" I asked.

"Most likely," he replied. He pinched my shoulder once

before letting go. "You should go home and rest, Emma. I believe you still have a case to finish."

Poor Buck. His fate was still hanging in the balance. And presumably Astrid was so preoccupied with the Knightsbridge family that she'd stopped the investigation into Walter's murder too. What a mess I'd created. I had to do everything in my power to clean it up.

"Thanks, I think I will." The prospect of sleeping in my own bed was very comforting. I took a step and paused, realizing that I'd hitched a ride with Astrid. "Would you mind giving me a lift home?" I was too tired to walk.

Lord Gilder displayed his fangs. "It would be my pleasure, sorceress."

CHAPTER 23

THE NEXT DAY I was determined to step back into my life and return to normal, whatever that was. I sent Sedgwick with a message early in the morning and then showed up at the office, ready to roll up my sleeves and get to work.

A latte from Brew-Ha-Ha waited on my desk when I arrived. I wrapped my hand around the cup. Still warm.

"Thanks, Althea," I called and heard a muffled reply from the room next door.

I opened Buck's file and began to read. I'd only made it halfway down the page when I heard a melodic voice outside the office door. Although I didn't recognize the song, I recognized the deep, throaty sound of the siren.

"Hi Alison," I said, as the door cracked open. "Thank you for coming."

The siren breezed into the room and drifted into the chair in front of my desk. "I got your message. Your owl has a real attitude, you know?"

"I do know." And was amazed that he could convey this attitude to Alison without words.

"Nice to be in this office again." Alison glanced around the room. "You haven't made too many changes, have you?"

"I forget you used to spend time here."

"Only if I wanted to see my workaholic fiancé." Alison was referring to her romantic relationship with Gareth. "How's my old flame? Still flickering?"

"He's great, actually. You should come by during the next séance and say hi."

She smiled. "I would like that very much. I do miss him."

"He'd be thrilled to talk to you again. I think he gets lonely, although he doesn't admit it."

She suppressed a smile. "That's the Scottish side of him. Repression." Her expression shifted to one of concern. "By the gods, he would have been lonely if you'd gone off to live with the Grey sisters or Raisa. I'm glad you came back."

"Between you and me, I wouldn't have lasted long in that cave. I like modern amenities too much."

"You're preaching to the converted." Alison eyed me carefully. "I take it you didn't ask me here to talk about the perils of cave life, though."

"Nope. I asked you here today to talk about the case against Buck."

Alison grimaced. "Ugh. Don't remind me about that. What do you want from me? You know as well as I do that I can't drop the charges since I'm not the one who brings them. It's the town."

"Oh, I know that," I said. "But you're also the prosecution's only witness. Without your testimony, they don't really have a case."

Alison cocked her head. "And why wouldn't they have my testimony? He peed all over my lawn and saw me half naked."

"And you saw him fully naked," I said.

Alison nodded emphatically. "Exactly. That's sexual harassment."

"You do realize that he only shifted back to human form because you startled him? He wasn't intending to flash you."

"It doesn't matter," Alison said firmly. "He broke the rules. He should be punished."

I sighed. This was going to be more difficult than I hoped.

"Do you know why he was drawn to your yard in the first place?" I asked.

"I've got a bed of peonies along the border. The werewolves seem to like the smell."

"Not peonies. He heard you singing through the open window. You were singing, weren't you?"

A dreamy smile touched her lips. "I'm always singing. It's my favorite thing to do and I'm damn good at it."

She'd get no argument from me. I'd heard her voice enough times to know that she was amazing.

"Buck heard your voice all the way from the forest. Before he even knew what he was doing, he found himself standing on your lawn listening to you. At that point he was desperate to pee, but he was unwilling to return to the woods while you were still singing." Some sirens led sailors to their watery graves with their voices. Alison led a werewolf to piss on her peonies.

"It was really because of my voice?" she queried. "I figured he was just a pervert."

I laughed. "I can't promise that he isn't that too. But he definitely was drawn to your yard because of your wonderful singing voice." I paused. "He also thinks you're very pretty."

Alison crossed her arms and glared at me. "Now you're just trying to butter me up so I agree not to testify."

I held up my hands, showing my palms. "I swear, Alison. I'm being one hundred percent honest. He doesn't even know I'm telling you this. He would probably be mortified. He likes to swagger and posture."

Alison chewed on a hangnail. "He is kind of cute, isn't he? I haven't had a date in a long time."

"I'm not saying you need to go out with him," I said. "But I think the shifters are working on getting these ordinances modified. They're not happy about the situation. I think if we could get the case against Buck dropped, it would go a long way toward soothing frayed nerves in the community."

"Who knew peeing on my lawn would get political?" Alison said with a hint of amusement. She stopped for a beat. "Okay, I'll tell Rochester that I won't testify. That I didn't see anything."

"Be careful how you frame it," I said. "The prosecution can coerce you to testify if they're determined to try this case." Although I doubted Rochester would. He was on my side when it came to modifying the excessive rules and regulations in Spellbound.

"So do me a favor," Alison said. "When's your next meeting with your client?"

"This afternoon, if my plan comes to fruition," I said.

"Tell him to knock on my door and say hi one of these days. He knows where I live." She stood and winked at me. "Thanks for the tip, Emma. You sure do know how to make a girl feel good."

"Pandora's got nothing on me," I said.

"If you ever get tired of this lawyering gig, you could always have a career in matchmaking."

"I love a good happily ever after," I said.

"Seems to me that you got one of your own," Alison replied.

"I did, didn't I?" The whole thing still seemed surreal. "I feel like the luckiest person in the world."

"Not a bad feeling, is it?" Alison said as she left the office.

No, it wasn't. Not at all.

. . .

Later in the afternoon I sat in Rochester's office, trying not to laugh at the mug on his desk. It had a picture of a kitten tangled up in a ball of yarn. It was so cute and out of character for the serious and intelligent wizard that I wondered whether someone gave the mug to him as a joke.

"You seem distracted, Emma," Rochester said. "You're not still worried about recent events, are you?"

I snapped to attention. "Oh no. Well, I'm a natural worry-wart, but I'm focused on my client's case."

"Is he in the reception area?" Rochester asked.

"Yes, flirting madly with your assistant."

"More like she's flirting with him. Kiki can't seem to help herself."

"That's a relief because I've been trying to set him up with Alison."

Rochester's eyes narrowed. "The siren whose lawn he peed on?"

Oops.

"Um, well..."

He tapped his fingers on the desk and regarded me carefully. "Is that the real reason she declined to testify? I was surprised to get her message earlier today."

I widened my eyes. "I have no idea what you're talking about."

He made a noise at the back of his throat and consulted the file in front of him. "Buck doesn't have any priors."

"No. Clean record. Reasonably well-liked in the community. The shifters have taken his arrest personally."

Rochester's brow furrowed. "I noticed. It's bad for community spirit, especially given the mayor's removal. We need to proceed with caution."

"I may have caused a few waves, too," I said. "Spellbound needs a period of calm."

Rochester drummed his fingers more quickly. "Without a witness, it will be hard to prove anything."

"True." I hesitated. "Do you want me to call in my client? Any questions you want to ask?"

Rochester cocked his head. "To be honest, Emma. I'm amazed you're sitting here right now. You must be mentally and emotionally exhausted."

I smoothed the front of my shirt. "I'm doing well. Thanks for asking."

"You don't want to take any time off from work?" he queried. "Maybe a vacation?"

"To where? Curse Cliff? Swan Lake? I've seen enough of both places recently."

He chuckled. "Yes, vacations spots are a little hard to come by in Spellbound."

"I'll be fine, Rochester. I appreciate your concern. I've had wonderful offers of support from friends. Lady Weatherby wants to keep me at the academy. I think coming to the office is good for me. Keeps me from spending too much time in my own head."

He nodded. "A dangerous place for anyone to dwell for too long, I think."

"You're a sensible guy, Rochester. Has anyone ever told you that?"

He straightened his tie. "You don't become a town prosecutor without a healthy dose of sensibility."

A thought occurred to me. "Have you ever considered running for mayor?"

"Mayor?" He seemed taken aback. "Me?"

"Why not you?"

His brow lifted as he absorbed the question. "I'd have to give it some thought, but my instinct would be no. I like being a lawyer. Running a town wouldn't be the same."

"Someone's going to have to step into Mayor Knights-bridge's shoes," I said.

"I think your friend Lucy is a good bet," he replied. "Everyone was happy with her performance during the youth spell crisis. We'll see how she performs as interim mayor."

"Lucy would be great," I agreed.

"As interesting as this conversation is, I suppose we shouldn't leave your client waiting," Rochester said.

I'd nearly forgotten about Buck. "Yes, of course. I'll get him." I hustled to the door and whistled for Buck to come in.

"Very professional," Rochester said with an amused smirk.

"He responds well to that sort of thing," I said.

"Whistling at him like a dog?" Rochester queried. "I should think he'd be offended."

Buck appeared in the doorway, anxiously twisting the edge of his shirt. "You got questions for me?"

"Have a seat, Mr. Testani," Rochester said.

"I'd rather stand if that's okay," Buck said. "I've been sitting for a while and my butt cheeks are numb."

"Very well." Rochester fixed Buck with his serious lawyer face. "It's my understanding that no one saw you relieve yourself on Alison's property."

"Uh, that's right," he said, shooting an uncertain look in my direction. "No one could have seen me because I didn't do it."

"Fine. Let's all agree that you relieved yourself in the forest before you reached the property line." Rochester smiled at me. "Satisfied?"

Buck glanced from Rochester to me. "That's it?"

"Not quite," I said. "Someone accidentally trampled Alison's peonies a couple of weeks ago. It might be worth stopping by the garden center and bringing her new ones. I think she'd like that."

Buck appeared surprised. "You think she'd like it if I brought them to her?"

I inclined my head. "Only one way to find out. Just make sure to use the restroom before you get there."

"Hardy har," he said. "That's funny, Miss Hart, especially since I would *never* use anything *but* a restroom. I'm a classy guy." He gave me an exaggerated wink and I heard Rochester strangle a laugh.

"I'm glad that's settled," Rochester said. "Now if you'll both excuse me, I have another meeting and I imagine Miss Hart is anxious to get home where a special someone might be waiting for her."

Truer words were never spoken.

CHAPTER 24

Lady Weatherby's dark eyes bore into mine. "There is no room for laziness in this classroom. Your power is too volatile, Miss Hart. Too dark."

We were alone in the classroom at the academy. My first of many private lessons with the head of the coven.

"Why does everyone assume that?" I asked. "That's not been my experience. I don't feel like this is negative energy in any way." In fact, it seemed exactly the opposite.

"Do not underestimate the power of dark magic," Lady Weatherby said. "It has a mind of its own. It can disguise itself. Fool an innocent." I felt the missing words at the end of her sentence. *Like you.*

"I'm not here to argue with you," I said. "I'm here to learn how to control the magic." So that the entire town didn't cower in my presence. "Tell me what to do and I'll do it."

Lady Weatherby's mouth quirked. "Very well then. Why don't we try a manifestation spell?"

"What's that?"

"A basic sorceress trick," Lady Weatherby explained. "It allows you to create something out of nothing."

"You mean like imagining my quill from home and bringing it here? But we learned that in remedial witch class."

Lady Weatherby shook her head and her headdress shifted slightly. "No, I'm not talking about an existing item within the town limits. I'm talking about *anything*."

"Anything?" I echoed. "Like an ugly yellow Hummer? Or a machine gun? Anything from the human world?"

"I believe starting small is the best way to learn," Lady Weatherby said. "We must be careful not to let the magic overtake you."

"So how do I do it? Do I just imagine it and hold out my hands?"

"You focus your will, same as in witchcraft. You draw from the magic deep inside yourself and envision the very thing you intend to pull here."

I knew exactly what I wanted to pull here. Excitement grew within me. Sorceress powers were amazing. So much better than remedial witchcraft, not that I'd admit it to my friends.

"Will you give Millie extra credit for mastering the invisibility and visibility spells?" I asked.

"Extra credit will not help her achieve the next level," Lady Weatherby replied. "And she's fortunate that you were unharmed. To be perfectly honest, I am still tempted to punish her for her arrogance."

"Please don't do that," I begged. "She did it to help me. You don't want to discourage her from helping others."

"Millie helps herself first," Lady Weatherby replied. Then added quietly, "That is one of the crucial differences between the two of you." She clapped her hands together. "Enough talk of Millie. Now close your eyes and focus."

I did as instructed. I pictured the owl, its familiar feathers. Its intelligent eyes. I held out my hands and focused my will.

What the hell? a familiar voice squawked.

My eyes flew open and I was shocked to see Sedgwick in my hands. He struggled against me and flew to the nearest perch.

What are you trying to do—kill me? I was mid-flight and now suddenly I'm here.

"I'm sorry, Sedgwick. It was an accident. I wasn't trying to summon you. I was trying to do a manifestation spell."

Well, try harder. You suck.

"Gee, thanks for the encouragement."

Do me a favor and open a window so I can get out of here unscathed, Sedgwick said.

I crossed the room and pushed up the nearest window, giving him plenty of room to fly through.

"I'm sorry. I'll try not to do it again." Poor Sedgwick. Wrong place and wrong time.

"I take it that was not your intention," Lady Weatherby said, assessing me.

"No, in fact…" Wrong place and wrong time. A spell gone awry. My eyes widened.

"Miss Hart, are you all right?"

My mouth dropped open. "I know what happened to Walter Rivers. I need to get to Astrid's office now."

"But our lesson," Lady Weatherby said. "It is important to make progress."

"But it's even more important to catch Walter's killer. He deserves closure and so do his loved ones." His multiple loved ones. I raced out the door before Lady Weatherby could stop me. We'd have to finish our lesson another time.

Luckily, Astrid was in her office when I arrived. I explained my theory and Astrid listened with her usual open mind.

"Let's go pick her up," Astrid said. "I know where she lives."

"What about Britta?" I asked. "Is she around?"

Astrid shook her head. "She's on meter maid duty today."

"Why? What did she do?"

Astrid smiled. "Actually, she requested it. She finds it calming. She seems to be all about an even keel these days."

No doubt harp therapy played in role in that.

"I'll go with you then," I said. "You might need backup."

"Suit yourself," Astrid said. "You know I always like your company."

We took the Sheriff's jalopy and drove to the southwest corner of town. A neighborhood called Oberon Hills.

"There she is now," I said. The fairy was on her front lawn, using her wand to try to keep a rubber ball in the air. It repeatedly dropped to the ground and then she'd attempt to raise it again. She couldn't seem to keep the ball airborne.

"Anya Applewhite," Astrid said, stepping out of the car. "Please lower your wand."

Anya stopped and stared at us. I could see from her expression that she knew exactly why we were here. Her grey eyes were awash with fear. That wasn't necessarily a good thing, not while she still held her wand.

"Please. It was an accident," Anya said, taking a step backward. She extended her wand toward us.

"Anya, please lower your wand," I said. "No one wants to hurt you. We only want to talk."

"Do you know how it feels to be expelled in front of everyone?" Anya asked, tears streaming down her cheeks. "Do you know how it feels to be the daughter of two skilled fairies and not be able to do a simple revival spell?"

"I know exactly how you feel," I said. "I'm in the remedial witch class at the academy, remember? When I told you that I had friends who were amazing but not in an academic setting, I meant it. My friend Sophie is a brilliant witch, but sometimes she's a bit clumsy and spells go awry. It doesn't make her a bad witch, though."

Anya remained firmly rooted to the ground with her wand pointed toward us. Her guard was up. Way up. I mentally prepared myself for an attack. I didn't want to end up like Walter.

"I went to the woods because I thought I would be alone to practice," Anya said. "Everyone else was in school, so I didn't expect anyone to be there. I didn't even hear him coming. I was so focused on trying to do the spell properly."

"Which spell were you trying to do?" Astrid asked.

"A revival spell," Anya said. "I messed it up so badly in class that they expelled me. They told my parents they had nothing to teach someone of my low caliber. I was devastated. But I was determined to show them they were wrong."

"If you were doing a revival spell," I said, "then why was Walter frozen to death?"

"I was freezing the flowers to death and then reviving them," Anya explained. "I only wanted to practice on the flowers so that I didn't hurt anything." She bit her lip. "He came across the bridge. I turned around when I heard the noise. I wasn't thinking about my wand, that I'd just done the spell. Instead of landing on the flower, it landed on the troll." She squeezed her eyes shut and began to cry in earnest.

"Anya, we believe you," Astrid said. "Place your wand on the ground and we can talk more about it."

"What will happen to me?" Anya cried. "Will I go to Spellbound Prison? This is murder, right?"

"Not necessarily," I said. "Accidental death is different, plus you're a minor. If you're convicted, it will carry less prison time."

Astrid beckoned her forward. "Come on, Anya. We know it was a mistake. You don't want to hurt anybody else and make it worse."

Anya looked uncertain, and I realized that her hand was shaking.

"Walter had a workshop in the woods not far from the bridge," I said. "He was coming home after visiting there. He made amazing inventions. He was a good troll and his loved ones deserve closure."

"I know," Anya said. "When he dropped dead, I tried to drag him off the bridge and revive him. I couldn't do it, though. A spell like that doesn't work on living, breathing paranormals, only things like flowers and trees. I dragged him as far as I could and tried a couple of spells, but nothing worked."

"Then why didn't you run for help?" Astrid asked. "If you had gone for help, then maybe he would've had a chance."

Anya collapsed on the ground in a heap. "I don't know. I'd just been expelled. I didn't want to make it worse. My parents have been so disappointed in me."

Well, they were going to feel more than disappointment now. Still, I found myself feeling sorry for Anya. She'd been subjected to so much pressure to achieve. It was no wonder she cracked.

Astrid advanced slowly toward the fairy, retrieving her wand from the grass beside her. "Anya Applewhite, I place you under arrest for the death of Walter Rivers."

It was then that Cindy Applewhite emerged from the house, looking confused. "Sheriff? What's going on?"

"You may want to come down to the office," Astrid said. "Your daughter will need an adult present."

That was the one thing Anya had going for her. She was still a minor. The sentencing guidelines would take that into account, even the existing tougher ones. Under the circumstances, it was the best she could hope for.

CHAPTER 25

I AWOKE RELUCTANTLY from the most wonderful dream. Daniel and I were in the dining room downstairs, having dinner with my parents. There was no special occasion. It was a typical evening where we ate roast beef with gravy and homemade biscuits and shared the trivial details of our day. It felt so *normal.* I treasured every fake moment of it.

I stretched my legs and arms before flipping back the covers and padding across the floor to the bathroom. Sometimes I didn't even make it through the night without a bladder break. I completely sympathized with Buck's urinary needs.

"Someone's in a good mood," Gareth said.

I glanced over my shoulder to see him hovering in the bathroom doorway. "Privacy, please."

"Since when?"

I grabbed a washcloth and began to scrub my face. "How do you know I'm in a good mood?"

"Because you're humming to yourself," he said. "You only hum when you're happy."

I stared at myself in the mirror. "Do I?" I'd never noticed.

"You get to know a lot about a person when you live together," Gareth said.

"Why do I feel like that statement is laced with meaning?" I went back to the business of washing my face.

Gareth shrugged. "Only an observation. Nothing to do at all with your budding romance of heavenly proportions."

I rounded on him. "It has everything to do with my budding romance. Gareth, are you worried that I'm going to move in with Daniel and leave you here alone?"

Gareth fixated on the floorboards. "No." He paused. "But I might be worried that Daniel will move in here. It would completely change the dynamic. This house is only large enough for one incredibly handsome male."

From out of nowhere, Magpie hissed his disapproval.

Gareth smiled. "Apologies. Two incredibly handsome males."

I barked a short laugh. "Let's not get ahead of ourselves. We've only gotten to the stage where we've admitted our feelings for each other. I don't think he'll be showing up on the front porch with his bags anytime soon."

The wind chimes jingled and Gareth and I exchanged an uneasy look.

"I'll suss it out," Gareth said and disappeared.

I hurriedly brushed my hair and tried to make myself presentable. Why would anyone turn up so early and so unexpectedly?

"Just as I feared," Gareth said, returning to my bedroom. "Daniel is here."

"Presumably without his suitcase."

"Aye."

I glanced down at my fuzzy pajama set. Not remotely sexy, but it would have to do.

"You're not going to open the door like that, are you?" Gareth asked.

I headed for the stairs, unconcerned. "He loves me, Gareth—old lady pajamas and all."

"It must be love," Gareth muttered. "There's no other excuse for that kind of tolerance."

I hustled down the steps and yanked open the front door. Sure enough, Daniel stood there, looking as handsome as ever in a pair of charcoal jeans and a body-hugging turquoise T-shirt that matched his eyes. His gossamer wings fanned out behind him. Seeing him again let loose a butterfly frenzy in my stomach. I couldn't imagine a day when my body didn't react to the sight of him.

"Good morning," Daniel said, grinning widely. "I'm so glad you're up. I didn't want to have to wake you, but I was willing."

"Do we have plans?" I asked. There was no way I would have forgotten making plans with Daniel.

"I was hoping we could spend the day together," he said. "I know it's short notice, but I feel like we've missed so much time together recently. I don't want to make that mistake again. Time is precious."

"Says the immortal," I quipped.

He took my hand. "I am, but you're not. And I don't want to waste a single moment on my own when I could be with you."

My heart fluttered. No one made me feel the way Daniel did. Like I was the most special snowflake in the blizzard. For someone with my tragic background, that took real talent.

"I'm happy to spend the day together," I said, "but I'd at least like to get dressed first."

Daniel stepped into the foyer. "No problem. I'm happy to wait. You deserve every ounce of my patience."

"Be back in a few," I said. I raced up the stairs and back to my bedroom where Gareth had already placed an outfit on the bed.

I marveled at him. "You were able to touch the hangers?"

He inclined his head. "Sometimes I surprise even myself."

I studied the outfit on the bed. As always, Gareth's taste was impeccable. "Thank you." I hesitated. "I was wondering if you'd be angry that I kept my secret from you."

"The sorceress thing?" Gareth queried.

"Not exactly a minor detail."

He waved me off. "I know all about keeping secrets from people I care about, Emma. You had your reasons and I respect that."

"It means a lot to me that you're being supportive."

"How could I not be supportive?" he asked. "You deserve every happiness, Emma. And I want to help you in any way I can. Dead or not, I still have a lot to offer."

"Of course you do," I said. I quickly changed my clothes and swilled my anti-anxiety potion.

"Have fun today," Gareth said. "I'll be here waiting for you."

Daniel was in the living room when I returned downstairs. He stood in front of the mantel, admiring the blue and yellow pot.

"That's from the Mad Potter, isn't it? We went there together when you first came here."

"Yes, it was your gift to me. I gave it pride of place in the house."

He smiled softly. "I hope it's the first of many gifts I'm able to give you."

I linked my arm through his. "I don't need gifts, Daniel. Not when I have you."

"It's a beautiful day," he said.

I laughed, feeling more light-hearted than I had in ages. "When isn't it a beautiful day in Spellbound?"

"Then let's not waste it."

"Where are we going?"

He bumped me gently with his elbow. "Does it matter?"

No. As long as we were together, it really didn't.

He waited until we were clear of the front porch to spread his wings to their full capacity. "Hop on."

I hesitated. "Are you sure?"

He pulled me toward him. "What's the worst that can happen?"

That list was far too long. "I puke on your gorgeous head?"

"Then I'll wash my hair. It'll be fine." He flapped his wings. "Let's go, Hart. While the sun is still shining."

I walked over to him and looped my hands around his neck. He lifted me into his arms and leaped into the air.

"Try not to strangle me," he choked out. I loosened my grip on his neck.

We flew over Spellbound and I forced myself to keep my eyes open and enjoy the passing scenery. The clock tower and the dramatic church spire. The Mayor's Mansion. The majestic forests and the hills in the distance. It was important not to go through life with my eyes closed and my walls up. Otherwise, I'd miss all the good stuff.

I knew where he was taking me before we even got there. We came up and over the cliff and landed gently on the cliff's edge. Swan Lake glistened below.

"Your Contemplate the State of the Universe spot?" I queried.

"It used to be," he said. "Then it became the place where I thought about you." He pointed to the road that ran along the other side of the lake. "That's where I first spotted that silly green car of yours."

I gave him a playful punch in the ribs. "Sigmund is not

silly. He's a wonderful car." And the last physical link I had to my grandparents.

"He'd better be. Do you know how difficult it was to get him out of the bottom of the lake?"

I stared at the place across the lake where my life changed forever. "Do you ever wonder what would've happened if I hadn't seen you up here? If I had kept driving?"

"All the time," he admitted. "I'm so grateful that you're a distracted driver."

I jerked my head to glare at him and saw the hint of a smile on his lips. "Daniel, that's not funny. I am not a distracted driver. I saw someone in need and I reacted."

He wrapped his strong arms around me and pulled me against his chest. I felt the soft, steady thump of his heartbeat reverberate between us.

"I was someone in need," he said. He tipped my chin upward. "I just didn't realize that what I needed was you."

I remained perfectly still as his lips met mine. It was the softest kiss I'd ever experienced, infused with more love than I'd ever hoped to feel.

"I'm so glad I found this place," I murmured.

He leaned down and pressed his forehead against mine. "Me too. It doesn't feel cursed anymore. Not since the day you showed up and turned this town upside down."

I pinched his waist and he laughed. "What if the curse was broken tomorrow? Would you leave?"

"That depends," he said, kissing me again. His fingers danced through strands of my hair.

"On what?" My whole body warmed, responding to his touch.

"On whether you wanted to stay or go."

"You'd leave your home to be with me?" Although I felt the same way, it was nice to know we were on the same page.

I'd follow Daniel to the heavens, with or without wings and a shiny halo.

"No, I wouldn't have to leave home," he replied.

I frowned. "Because you think I'd stay?"

Daniel smiled and cupped my cheeks with his hands. "No, because home is wherever you are."

"Ditto," I said, and kissed him again for good measure.

Thank you for reading *Cast Away*! For information on sales and new releases, sign up for my newsletter via my website at www.annabelchase.com and like me on Facebook.

Grab *A Touch of Magic*, the next book in the series!

More series by Annabel Chase

Starry Hollow Witches

Federal Bureau of Magic

Midnight Empire

Pandora's Pride

Divine Place

Magic Bullet

Hex Support Mystery

Made in the USA
Las Vegas, NV
26 December 2023